"Guess we made it through the night more or less unscathed, huh?"

Shannon followed Gideon's gaze and released a soft sigh. The cool morning breeze off the gulf lifted her dark hair, sending a few strands dancing against his cheeks. She smelled like a fresh morning rain, despite having traipsed through the sea grass, climbed up and down a thirty-foot lighthouse and taken down a special forces marine twi⸺ ⸺ize with her bare hands.

She was formidable ⸺ ⸺ around in his head ⸺

Fearing it.

He'd known, the sec⸺ ⸺ waiting on the pier at Terrebonne M⸺ ⸺, that she was going to be trouble for him.

He just hadn't realized how much.

PAULA GRAVES

SECRET ASSIGNMENT

HARLEQUIN®
entertain, enrich, inspire™

For my mom,
who's always believed in me, even when I didn't.

Recycling programs
for this product may
not exist in your area.

ISBN-13: 978-0-373-69633-8

SECRET ASSIGNMENT

ABOUT THE AUTHOR

Alabama native Paula Graves wrote her first book, a mystery starring herself and her neighborhood friends, at the age of six. A voracious reader, Paula loves books that pair tantalizing mystery with compelling romance. When she's not reading or writing, she works as a creative director for a Birmingham advertising agency and spends time with her family and friends. She is a member of Southern Magic Romance Writers, Heart of Dixie Romance Writers and Romance Writers of America.

Paula invites readers to visit her website, www.paulagraves.com.

Books by Paula Graves

HARLEQUIN INTRIGUE

*Cooper Justice
**Cooper Justice: Cold Case Investigation
‡Cooper Security

CAST OF CHARACTERS

Shannon Cooper—Though Cooper Security's computer tech has long wanted to run a field operation, helping a widow archive her late husband's belongings isn't what she had in mind—until black-masked intruders show up, pursuing a deadly agenda.

Gideon Stone—Owing a blood debt to the family of the fellow marine who died saving his life, Gideon will do anything to keep Lydia Ross safe, even put up with a pretty young computer geek who wastes no time getting under his tough skin.

Lydia Ross—The army widow is still grieving the loss of her husband and her son. But when intruders strike the private Gulf of Mexico island where she's lived for most of her life, she shows the steel in her spine that made her the ideal army wife.

General Edward Ross—The late army general kept a coded journal during his last few years of service. Now a whole lot of dangerous people want to get their hands on the journal. What secrets does it contain?

Security Services Unit (SSU)—MacLear Security's secret unit disbanded when the company fell to scandal. But some of the operatives are still selling their services to whomever's willing to pay.

Damon North—The undercover agent has finally made his way back into the SSU, dedicated to bringing the dangerous mercenary unit down. But how far is he willing to go to convince the unit that he's trustworthy?

Raymond Stephens—The dishonorably discharged ex-marine who found his home in the corrupt SSU still nurses a grudge against Gideon Stone. Will the new SSU mission to steal the general's journal give him a chance to even the score?

Chapter One

Murky green water lapped against the pilings of the Terrebonne Marina docks, rocking the boats hitched to the moorings. The breeze blowing in from the Gulf of Mexico was steamy-hot, fueled by temperatures in the mid-nineties and eighty-percent humidity.

August in Alabama, Shannon Cooper thought bleakly as she wilted in the sweltering heat on a bench by an empty boat slip. The dog days were bad enough back home, where mountains and woods offered some small protection against the Southern summer's excesses. But down here in Terrebonne, a mosquito-infested dot on the Alabama Gulf Coast map, August was a ruthless son of a—

She heard the boat before she saw it, the engine rattle drawing her gaze toward the middle of Terrebonne Bay. Cutting through the wakes left by other boats, a drab white fishing yacht that had seen better days headed straight toward the boat slip where she sat waiting for her ride to Nightshade Island.

The boat eased into the slip, avoiding all but the lightest of bounces against the protective bumpers lining the dock. The engine growled to a stop, and Shannon pushed to her feet.

A colossus of a man stepped onto the deck, all broad shoulders, long legs and unwelcoming scowl. Shannon was used to large men—between her brothers and cousins, she'd been surrounded by strapping, athletic men all her life. But the man

who walked to the boat's deck railing exuded a command-
ing presence made all the more intimidating by the impatient hostility hardened like stone in his masculine features.

He didn't speak until he'd finished lashing the boat to
the moorings with sturdy ropes. That task done, he rose to
his impressive height and addressed her in a deep, growling
Southern drawl. "Shannon Cooper?"

She quelled the dismay squirming in the pit of her stomach and raised her chin. "Yes. And you?"

His lips pressed to a line. "Gideon Stone."

The name matched the one her brother had given her. She
wished Jesse had thought to include a photo of the man. "Do
you have any identification?"

His eyes narrowing, he pulled a slim wallet from the back
pocket of his jeans and showed her his driver's license. Gideon
Stone. Age thirty-four. Six-five, 220 pounds. In the photo, he
looked pissed-off.

She glanced at him and saw the photo was a good likeness.
"Thank you," she said politely.

His expression didn't soften at all as his gaze shifted downward. "Is that all you have?"

She looked at the duffel bag sitting on the dock beside her.
She'd packed light, figuring she could wash clothes at least
once while she was on the island. "Doesn't Mrs. Ross have
a washer and dryer?"

His eyebrows quirked slightly. "Yes."

"Then yes. That's all I have." She eyed the large fishing
vessel, a Hatteras Convertible Sportfisherman. Even though
it had seen better days, it seemed in no danger of sinking,
she noted with relief.

"Are you sure you want to do this?"

She blinked, taken aback. "Do this?"

"Come out to Nightshade Island." He nodded toward the
clouds rolling in from the southeast. "There's a storm headed
our way."

A tropical storm roiling in the Caribbean was lining up to move into the Gulf of Mexico before the end of the week, but surely they would have plenty of time to evacuate if the situation became dangerous. "All the more reason to archive the general's papers and collections quickly," she said reasonably. "Mrs. Ross will want to take them with her if she's forced to evacuate, and we'll have them secured and ready to go. Were you able to procure the items we requested for storage?"

"Yes." He walked toward the dockside fuel pump a few yards away.

She watched through narrowed eyes as he pumped fuel into the yacht's tanks, wondering if his surly attitude was situational or inherent. "Is there a problem with my coming here?"

He looked up at her, his eyes hooded. "Should there be?"

Well, that was a strange response. "I don't think so. You do know Mrs. Ross hired us to help her itemize her husband's things and pack them up securely for the move, right?"

"Right." But he sounded suspicious anyway.

She sighed and picked up the duffel bag, shoving it over the rail onto the boat deck. If she had been dressed in shorts and a T-shirt—her preferred attire on scorching days—she'd have hauled herself over the deck railing as well. But she'd dressed to give a good first impression, although perspiration had already begun soaking through the cotton of her sleeveless shell and no doubt had left dark stains on the back of her light gray summer suit jacket.

Besides, she doubted she could have worn anything that would impress Gideon Stone.

She walked around to the back of the boat where a set of low steps gave her a more dignified entry to the boat. The boat's name was painted there, in straight blue letters. *Lorelei*.

She darted a glance at Gideon Stone, wondering for the first time if the boat belonged to Mrs. Ross or to him. She tried to picture the grim boat pilot as the sort of romantic who'd name a boat after a lover but gave up quickly.

Her brother had given her a job to do. It might be boring grunt work, but she was going to do it as well as she'd ever done anything in her life. Then maybe he'd take her contributions to Cooper Security more seriously and let her take part in more challenging assignments.

Gideon finished fueling up and nodded toward the steps. "We're ready to shove off."

"Want me to get the other rope?" she asked as he bent to unlash the back rope from the mooring.

"I'll get it." His tone set her teeth on edge.

Once the boat was untied, he showed her into the cabin on the main deck, waving toward a worn but comfortable-looking L-shaped sofa inside. "There are life jackets in the cabinets under the sofa if you need one. You do know how to use one?"

She forced herself to smile as if his gruff manner didn't make her want to swat him. "Practically grew up in a marina." She'd spent half her childhood at Cooper Cove Marina with her aunt and uncle while her father was on duty with the sheriff's department.

The cabin was larger than it looked from outside, though perhaps the illusion of space was a result of its well-placed accommodations. The sofa ran the length of the port side, while a long set of storage cabinets lined the starboard, ending where a small but well-appointed galley took up the rest of the wall space. Gideon waved his large hand toward the small refrigerator. "There's bottled water and soft drinks in the cooler. Mrs. Ross thought you might need something to drink on a day like today."

His tone suggested he couldn't care less about her comfort, and he didn't stick around to make sure she found something to her liking, heading out to the deck without another word. He went straight up the ladder to the pilothouse overhead.

"Lovely meeting you, too, Mr. Stone." She shrugged off the jacket of her lightweight suit and crossed to the nearest air vent, sighing with pleasure as the cold air blew across her sticky skin. The boat surged under her feet, knocking her temporarily off balance. She caught herself, flattening her hand on the wall until she felt steadier. Keeping contact with the wall in case the boat hit any choppy water as it crossed the bay, she circled to the refrigerator and opened the door, smiling at the sight of several bottles and cans chilling inside.

Her sweet tooth argued for a soft drink, but her good sense went straight for the bottled water. She waited until she reached the bench before she opened it, saving herself a small mess when the boat lurched again just as she was taking her seat.

Good thing she didn't get seasick, she thought. Not that Gideon Stone had even asked if she might.

She pulled up the shade over the windows and saw land growing more and more distant as they moved out of the sheltered bay and into the choppier waters of the Gulf of Mexico. She wished the surly boat captain hadn't more or less ordered her to sit down and stay put. Now that she'd had a chance to cool down and rehydrate, she'd love to be outside, taking in the panoramic view of the Gulf.

Who says you have to listen to ol' Growly Gus? a rebellious voice whispered in her ear. The water wasn't much choppier than a windy day on Gossamer Lake, and she'd ridden out those kinds of swells in less sturdy boats than the *Lorelei*.

Why not?

The breeze blowing off the Gulf was cooler out here than it had felt back on the dock, countering the blistering afternoon heat. The cloud cover starting to gather overhead showed no sign of dropping moisture yet, and now that she had her sea legs under her, the walk across the deck to the railing posed no problem at all.

She glanced upward and saw Gideon Stone sitting in the pilothouse, his back to her as he steered the boat into the open water of the Gulf. She craned her neck to see around the bulk of the boat cabin, wondering if Nightshade Island was in sight yet.

She knew from studying a map of the coast that Nightshade Island was a tiny speck of land barely visible on the map of the Alabama Gulf Coast. From preparatory research in the library and online, Shannon had learned the island had belonged to the Stafford family for over a hundred years, passed down generation to generation until it finally fell in the hands of the only remaining member of the original family, Lydia Stafford Ross.

According to Jesse, who'd spoken to Mrs. Ross when he took the assignment for Cooper Security, Mrs. Ross and her husband, U.S. Army General Edward Ross, had lived there most of their married life, although the general had obviously spent a good deal of time away during his military career. "It was his home base," Jesse had told her. "He kept all his papers, correspondence and collections there."

Lydia Ross, he'd explained, had agreed to the State of Alabama's latest offer to purchase the island as a wildlife preserve, so she needed Cooper Security's help archiving and securing the general's belongings for the move.

Jesse had tried to make it sound like the best field assignment available, but Shannon knew when someone was throwing her a bone. Clearly her brother was tired of her nagging him to let her out from behind her computer screen and this was his punishment.

"You didn't like the accommodations?"

Stone's voice, closer than expected, made her jump. She gripped the railing, fighting a sudden rush of vertigo as she lost her sense of equilibrium. It returned quickly, however, and the world righted beneath her feet.

Squinting against the bright sunlight, she spotted Gideon Stone at the back edge of the pilothouse, gazing down at her. He loomed there, enormous and imposing.

"No, everything's fine." She shielded her eyes with her hand. "Is the island in sight yet?"

He hesitated before answering. "Come up. The view's better."

He said no more, turning back to the wheel and sitting in the pilot's chair. She scurried up the ladder before he changed his mind and took the seat beside him.

The view from the pilothouse *was* better, a 360-degree panorama of Gulf water ahead and shoreline disappearing behind them. In the distance, Shannon spotted a speck of dark green on the hazy turquoise horizon. "Is that Nightshade Island?"

Gideon didn't answer, gazing at the instrument gauges with a frown on his face. This time she sensed his expression had nothing to do with her.

She followed his gaze to the gauges and didn't see anything alarming, but now that she thought about it, their speed had slowed noticeably. "Is something wrong?"

"I don't know." He throttled back until they were just idling, then cut the engine.

She shot him a wary look, beginning to wonder if coming onto a boat with a strange man had been her smartest move. "What are you doing?"

"Fuel's not getting to the engine. I need to find out why."

"Are we stranded? Should we radio the Coast Guard?"

"Not yet. It may be something easily fixed." He got up from the pilot's chair and headed down the ladder.

"Do I need to go get my life jacket now?"

He paused, just his head and shoulders visible now. "We're not sinking." He kept climbing down.

"Yet," she muttered.

She eased over to the pilot's seat and found it still warm from Gideon's body. An odd tingle of feminine awareness jittered through her, making her feel vulnerable and intrigued at the same time.

She liked big men. Tall men, men with broad shoulders and strong backs. Men with battle-hardened faces and feral intensity. She knew such men were good to have around when the world went crazy.

But she also knew such men could be very, very dangerous. *Which are you, Gideon Stone?*

She looked around the pilothouse and spotted a small olive drab canvas bag sitting next to the console. It lay partially open.

Looking inside it would be wrong. She knew that. Gideon's private possessions were just that—private. And maybe if she weren't stranded at the moment on a boat with a man she'd met less than an hour earlier, she'd mind her own business and let it lie.

But her skin still prickled with wariness, and ignoring her healthy fear would be stupid.

She crouched next to the bag and carefully nudged it open until she could see the contents. Inside were a small first aid kit in a blue canvas pouch marked with a white cross, a couple of protein bars and, in the gloomy depths of the bag, the unmistakable outline of a Walther P99 pistol.

Shannon sat back on her heels, her heart pounding.

ONE LOOK AT the water trap of the engine's water separator filter and Gideon's heart sank. It was full.

Sitting back on his heels, he wiped sweat from his forehead with his sleeve. He'd fitted the system with a new water separator filter the evening before. He'd checked the bowl of the water trap, too, and it had been clean of all but a small amount of condensation.

No way had this much water collected overnight from mere condensation.

Think, Stone. Think.

He heard footsteps above, distant enough to reassure him that the woman was still up in the pilothouse, but also a reminder he was about to take a stranger to Nightshade Island, a stranger he wasn't sure he should trust. She'd be sleeping under Mrs. Ross's roof, where he couldn't watch her every second.

He'd heard of Cooper Security, but only in passing from an old Marine Corps buddy who'd known the company's CEO. Greg had assured him Jesse Cooper was a good man—a good marine. Under any other circumstances, his buddy's word might have been enough for Gideon.

But bad things had been going down recently, starting with General Ross's death.

The initial judgment was that the single-car crash just north of Terrebonne that had taken the general's life had been an accident. But the Terrebonne Sheriff's Department had recently assigned a detective to the accident investigation, which suggested that no matter what the official stance was at the moment, local law enforcement thought there might be more to it.

Gideon had thought so from the beginning. Edward Ross had been the most careful, conscientious driver he'd ever known. And at seventy years old, he'd still had the reflexes and physical stamina of a man twenty years his junior. The idea that the general had misjudged a curve in the middle of the afternoon was entirely unbelievable.

He drained the water from the trap into a bailing bucket. Then, on a hunch, he removed the hose from the electric fuel pump and let the contents of the fuel tank drain slowly into the bucket.

More water, he saw, anger battling dismay. Too much water.

Definitely not just condensation.

The bucket was over half full before the liquid flowing into it switched over from water to fuel. Since water was heavier than diesel, it had poured out first, which meant that most of what remained in the tank should be fuel. More than enough to get them back to the dock to refuel.

He returned the fuel pump hose to its proper position and covered the bucket with a plastic lid to keep the contaminated water from spilling. Still mulling over the implications of the excess water, he removed the saturated water replacement filter and went to the storage bin nearby to get the replacement filter he'd stored there a couple of months ago.

It wasn't there.

He knew it had been in the bin last night when he checked the boat for this afternoon's planned trip to the mainland. He hadn't checked right before the trip because he'd been running hard all morning, helping Mrs. Ross prepare her house for Shannon Cooper's arrival.

He left the engine well and climbed the steps to the main cabin, suffering a brief moment of suspense before he found a box of supplies—a few brand-new filters included—where he'd left them a couple of days ago when he'd gone out on a supply run.

As he refitted the engine with a replacement filter, he retraced his steps from the night before. System checks. Checked for life jackets in the benches. Checked oil levels, fuel levels. He'd checked the water trap for condensation, finding damn little even after almost three days of disuse.

He'd checked the supply cabinet to make sure the spare filter was there, damn it. He always made sure he kept spares of anything vital because that's what marines did—hoped for the best and prepared for the worst. And if it hadn't been there, he'd have grabbed one of the new filters and put it in the cabinet so it would be close at hand.

But clearly, he hadn't prepared well enough. He should have put some sort of early warning system on the boathouse, at the very least, to make sure nobody could tamper with the boat while he wasn't around.

Of course, the more pressing question was, why *had* someone tampered with the fuel? It wouldn't pose a particularly dangerous situation; the worst it could do was strand him on the water, and even if the radio had been sabotaged, there was enough boat traffic to ensure he wouldn't stay stranded long. Simple vandalism made no sense as an explanation—maybe if the boat were docked somewhere on shore where there was easy access to someone on foot or in a car. But to sabotage the *Lorelei* docked out on Nightshade Island, someone would have had to take a boat well out from the mainland, make a no-engine approach and sneak into the boathouse.

No vandalism was worth that effort.

Which left…

He checked his cell phone. No bars. With a sigh, he headed upstairs to the cabin and crossed to the satellite phone attached to the wall near the galley. Lydia Ross answered on the second ring. "Gideon, I was just thinking of you. I forgot to pick up any cherries when we were in town, and I so wanted to cook a cherry crumble for our guest."

"We're already behind schedule, Mrs. Ross, and I'm—" He stopped before he said he was heading back to the dock to refuel. Even considering the bucket of water he'd drained from the tank, he had plenty to go back and forth from the island to the dock. Refueling could wait.

He felt the strong urge to head back to the island immediately.

"I'm already halfway back," he finished. "Look out your bedroom window and you should be able to see us coming soon." He paused in the middle of the room, taking a look around. Shannon Cooper's suit jacket still lay on the bench where she'd apparently discarded it earlier. On the table in the galley sat an empty water bottle.

A couple of feet away sat her duffel bag. His gaze settled there and he moved forward, ducking to keep from bumping his head on the cabin's low ceiling.

"Oh, I must admit I look forward to having company. I've

let myself become quite the recluse." Lydia's soft laugh was rueful. "Is she as nice as she sounded on the phone?"

"She seems very nice," he said carefully, wondering if Shannon's innocent face hid a devious mind.

Because there was another possibility he hadn't considered.

What if Shannon had gone below deck after he'd left her in the cabin? She could have dumped a few bottles of water in the tank in no time through the access hatch, if she knew anything about boat engines.

Practically grew up in a marina...

"Mrs. Ross, why don't you go up to the widow's walk?" he suggested. From the large railed-in square of space on the roof of the house, she'd have a largely unobstructed few of the whole island. "You can look for us from there."

"Gideon, is something the matter?"

He sighed. Despite her gentle manner, Lydia Ross was as savvy as her husband had been, and just as tough in her more refined way. "Mrs. Ross, someone's sabotaged the boat. I've fixed the problem for now, but I'm worried it may have been an attempt to keep me off the island for a while."

"I see." He heard steel in her voice. "Shall I get the Remington?"

"I believe you should," he answered, quietly unzipping the duffel bag. Inside, beneath a tablet computer, he found neatly rolled sets of clothing. Everything inside smelled good, like fresh rain on a hot day. "I'm on my way, but go to the widow's walk and call if you see any boats trying to come ashore."

"Will do. I'll call back." As she hung up, Gideon froze, his gaze locked on the sleek, black subcompact GLOCK G26 tucked in the bottom of Shannon Cooper's bag.

She'd come aboard armed.

"What the hell do you think you're doing?"

Shannon Cooper's voice, close behind him, made his heart

skitter. He dropped the bag and turned toward her. "Do you sneak on purpose or does it just come—" He stopped cold.

She was holding his Walther in her right hand, barrel pointing down.

"What are you doing with that?"

"This?" She brought the pistol up, still pointing away from him. As he watched with racing pulse, she checked the chamber with easy skill. "I thought I'd ask you the same thing."

Chapter Two

Shannon's bravado was fading fast, but if there was anything she'd learned how to do in a houseful of rough-and-tumble siblings, it was to show no fear. "I want to know what's going on. Who were you just talking to?"

"I beg your pardon?"

"On the phone, just now. Who were you talking to? You said 'call me if you see any boats coming ashore.' Ashore at Nightshade Island? What are you up to?" She nodded toward her duffel bag, lying open on the floor. "Why were you going through my bag?"

"Put the gun down."

She shook her head. "I'll keep the Walther." But she lowered her hand again. "I'm not here to hurt anyone. I'm here to do a job. But I don't know you from Adam, and I don't like your snooping through my things."

"Back at you."

"*Your* bag was lying open."

"Fine. I'll rephrase. I don't like being interrogated at gunpoint."

She laid the Walther on the top of the cabinet nearest her. "Better?"

"I carry a gun for protection. Why do you carry one?"

So he'd seen the GLOCK. "Same reason. I have a license."

"So do I."

All her family had concealed carry licenses. She supposed it wouldn't be unusual for a former marine to have one as well. "That still doesn't answer my question. Who were you talking to?"

"Lydia Ross. I asked her to go to the high point of the house and look around to see if there was any unusual boat activity around the island." He took a couple of steps toward her. Slow and steady, as if he were being careful not to spook her.

She was spooked anyway. "Why would you think there might be?"

He moved closer still, his big body looming in the small cabin. He barely had headroom at all, his hair brushing the top of the cabin. He would have to duck to get through the door, she realized. But he could do a lot of damage to her if he wanted.

Did he want to?

"Because someone sabotaged the boat."

A chill washed over her. "How?"

"Don't you know?"

The conversation was careening off into unexpected territory. "How would I know?"

He took another step. A long one, bringing him only a few inches from her. His nearness seemed to steal the air from the boat cabin, leaving her feeling light-headed and sluggish. "Someone put at least a half gallon of water in the fuel tank, no doubt in an effort to strand this boat out in the middle of the Gulf. I didn't do it. But I left you in here for several minutes. All you'd have had to do is grab some of the bottled water in the fridge, go down to the engine room and add the water to the tank through the access port."

"I wouldn't know a fuel tank from a fish tank," she said flatly.

"You said you grew up in a marina."

"I said I practically grew up in a marina. Which means I know my way around a fishing boat, sure. But nobody ever let me mess with the engines. And they were mostly outboards anyway." She cocked her head. "You think I'm trying to keep you away from the island so someone else can—do what? Have there been threats to Mrs. Ross?"

Gideon backed away from her a few inches, his blue eyes narrowed to slits. "She's a wealthy woman. She owns things of value."

The picture became a little clearer. "You're not just the caretaker at the island, are you? You're her bodyguard."

His grim mouth curved a little, carving a surprising dimple in his cheek. "Just don't let her hear you say that."

She dragged her gaze away from the dimple and tried to gather her suddenly scattered thoughts. "You think someone's trying to keep you away from the island so Mrs. Ross will be more vulnerable?"

"I think we need to get back to the island. Now."

She stepped aside when he moved forward, bracing herself as he reached for the Walther on the table where she'd placed it. But he just slipped it into the waistband of his jeans.

He stooped under the door and turned to look at her. "You coming?"

"Can I bring my GLOCK?"

His lips curved, triggering the dimple again. "Do you know how to use it?"

She gave him a withering look that only spread his smile so that the other side of his face formed a dimple as well.

"Do what you want," he said, and headed up the ladder.

She grabbed her GLOCK, still in its holster, and clipped the whole thing to her hip. At the last minute, she went back to the galley and grabbed a couple of bottled waters, tucking them under one arm as she climbed one-handed up to the pilothouse.

"Here," she offered, holding out one of the bottles to him. "I counted, by the way. Five bottles of water left. I drank one earlier and here's two more. Eight total. How many did you put in the fridge?"

"Eight," he admitted.

Suddenly a low moaning wail rose in the air, distant but loud. Beside her, Gideon Stone tensed, his features hardening.

"What is that?" she asked.

"Trouble," he answered. He grabbed a phone receiver built into the instrument panel and dialed. "What's wrong?" Anger darkened his face, ice forming in his blue eyes as the person on the other end of the call answered. "Are you sure?"

Shannon tamped down her impatience, peering in the direction of the noise. She realized she could see the island now, a dark mass in the middle of the murky gray-green of the Gulf. It was no more than two miles in length and, from the looks of it, even narrower in width.

The noise was coming from somewhere on the island.

Gideon hung up the phone and reached into his bag, pulling out a pair of binoculars.

"Was that Mrs. Ross? What's happened? What's that sound?"

"It's a foghorn on the lighthouse on the western side of the island—see it there?" He pointed dead ahead. Sure enough, she saw a tall white lighthouse rising above the tree line. "It's not in use anymore, but the horn still works. I don't like leaving Mrs. Ross alone on the island, but sometimes I have to, so I had someone rig the power connection from the horn to go to the main house. Mrs. Ross can trigger the horn from the house now. You can hear it all the way to the mainland."

"Why did she trigger it?"

"There was a boat attempting a landing. Rubber raft, really, with an outboard motor. She saw it from the widow's walk on top of the house. So she ran and sounded the horn." He swung his binoculars in an arc, apparently looking for the offending boat. "She said they turned back around and started hightailing it away."

"Is that unusual?"

He lowered the binoculars to look at her. "We get trespassers," he admitted. "They don't always know the island is private. Sometimes you get people having boat trouble."

"Could today's incident have been something like that?"

His mouth tightened. "Maybe."

"But you don't think so."

He didn't answer, settling back in the pilot's seat and starting the boat engine. To Shannon's relief, the engine rumbled to life easily enough.

By the time they neared the island, the siren had died away to nothing. They rounded the southern tip of the island and aimed north toward the mouth of a cavernous boathouse. It had to have been built specifically for the Hatteras Convertible, Shannon thought. "How long have the Rosses owned this boat?" she asked as Gideon eased the boat into the shelter.

The interior of the boathouse was dark and shadowy, as if they'd gone from noon to twilight in a matter of seconds. Her eyes, accustomed to the bright sunlight bouncing off the water of the Gulf, had trouble dealing with the sudden darkness, making her temporarily blind.

Out of the gloom, Gideon's answer rumbled like thunder. "I don't know. It was here when I came."

With sunlight through the entrance driving away the worst of the shadows, Shannon's sight soon adjusted. She followed Gideon Stone down the ladder to the main deck and gathered her things.

"You might want to put away the GLOCK," Gideon suggested. "Mrs. Ross is probably already on edge."

Shannon unclipped the holster from her waistband and put the weapon and holster in her duffel bag. Gideon took the bag from her hands as if he were picking up a child's toy. He slung it over his shoulder and nodded for her to precede him down the pier.

Where the pier ended, a river stone walkway began, winding through lush, tree-shaded grass uphill toward a large house near the top of a small rise. "Stafford House," Gideon said quietly behind her. "Stafford is Mrs. Ross's maiden name. The island has been in her family for generations."

"And the house?" she asked, though she knew the answer.

"The old one was badly damaged by Hurricane Frederick decades ago, when Mrs. Ross's parents were still alive. They rebuilt to make it more hurricane-proof. I'm told the house looks exactly as it did before. Just taller." He withdrew his gaze from the house and looked at her, his mouth curving too slightly to trigger the dimples again. "Hope you're not afraid of heights. The bedrooms are on the top floor."

Stafford House gave the impression of a stately manor, with tall white columns supporting the front portico as well as the balcony on the top floor. Where the roof gable met at a point above the second floor, a widow's walk ringed the entire roof area. "Is that how Mrs. Ross spotted the intruders?" she asked as they reached the front walkway. The river stones here were edged by monkey grass and unlit walkway lanterns. Shannon imagined it would be lovely at night with the lights on.

"Yes," Gideon answered tersely.

The front door opened and a small woman in her late sixties walked out onto the long front veranda, a smile on her face. She must have been a stunner in her youth, Shannon thought, as elegant and lovely as she remained in her later years. She wore a short-sleeved cotton blouse in pale yellow and a pair of denim capri pants that showed off slim, smooth ankles.

"You must be Shannon." She held out her hands in welcome.

Shannon took the older woman's hands. "Mrs. Ross, it's nice to meet you. Your home is absolutely beautiful."

Lydia Ross smiled with pleasure at the compliment. "It will be heartbreaking to leave it behind. But the gentlemen with the Department of Conservation and National Resources have assured me that they plan to work with the Gulf Coast Historic Trust to preserve the house as a museum for visitors to the island."

Thinking about the family home back in Gossamer Ridge, the shabby but well-loved house where her father had raised his six boisterous children, Shannon felt a twinge of sympathy for Lydia's plight. Her father's home was no longer the place she lived, but it was still home to her, a place to which she knew she could retreat if she needed.

"Where will you live when you leave here?" she asked as Lydia showed her inside the house.

"My sister-in-law owns a farm in Burkettville. Her husband died a few years ago, and I know she's missing him terribly. Perhaps we'll be able to give each other some relief from the loneliness." She smiled. "It will be lovely to be around my nieces and nephews more."

Lydia's words sounded sincere, but in her eyes Shannon saw anxiety, as if she feared what further changes her future might hold.

There was no foyer inside, as she'd expected, only a large, airy room that seemed to spread all the way from the front of the house to the back. It was part living room, part dining room, with a large, airy kitchen near the back and, through several sets of French doors, a long veranda that overlooked a raised garden.

"Gideon, dear, I've given Shannon the blue room." As Gideon headed up the stairs to the top floor, Lydia turned to Shannon with a smile. "You don't mind if I call you Shannon, do you? And you must call me Lydia." She lowered her voice. "I've tried to get Gideon to call me by my given name as well, but he's so formal! My husband said it was because he was a marine."

Shannon smiled back. "Two of my brothers were marines. I know exactly what you're talking about."

Lydia showed her into the kitchen, where a small tray of cheese and crackers sat on the narrow breakfast bar, along with a pitcher of iced tea. "I hope you like sweet tea. I can come up with some soft drinks if you prefer."

"Tea is perfect." Shannon sat where Lydia indicated and took a couple of crackers and some slices of Havarti cheese from the tray. "Is it okay if I get started this afternoon? Going through your husband's papers, I mean."

Lydia looked surprised. "I thought you'd want to rest and start fresh in the morning."

"I'll do whatever you wish," Shannon said quickly, reading Lydia's reluctance. "We can spend this afternoon getting to know each other if that's what you prefer."

Lydia smiled ruefully. "I'm quite transparent, aren't I? It is rare for me to have female companionship these days. I haven't ventured to the mainland for more than a couple of hours at a time since Edward's death. It's hard to know how to deal with old friends—sometimes, I feel as if they're watching me carefully in anticipation of a breakdown."

Shannon impulsively put her hand atop Lydia's where it lay on the counter. "My sister lost her husband a few years ago, and she used to think the same thing. She didn't even like to be around the family sometimes because of it. But it wasn't what we were thinking, I promise. We just wanted to help her however she needed it."

Tears brimmed in Lydia's eyes, but she held on to them, as if refusing to let them fall. "And did you help her?"

Shannon smiled. "As much as she'd let us. But there's a happy ending—she remarried a week ago."

"Well, lovely for her!" Lydia's smile looked genuine. "The young are not meant to be alone."

"I don't think anyone's meant to be alone."

Lydia patted her hand. "I am fortunate, then, to have a kind young man like Gideon to keep me company, no?"

As if speaking his name conjured him into appearing,

Gideon came down the stairs and entered the kitchen with long, floor-eating strides. "I need to do a patrol of the island," he said tersely. "If you need me, I'll have the two-way with me."

"Thank you, dear. You're too good to me."

An odd, pained look flashed in Gideon's blue eyes before he nodded goodbye and headed back through the front door.

"How did Mr. Stone come to be your caretaker?" Shannon asked curiously, seeing an answering pain in her hostess's eyes.

Lydia smiled, but there was anguish in her expression. "My son died saving his life."

ABOUT A QUARTER mile north of the house, Gideon found the spot on the beach where the raft had tried to come ashore. Something like a Zodiac would be able to accommodate a crew of four, the number of men Mrs. Ross had seen from the widow's walk. It would also fit Mrs. Ross's description of the vessel she'd seen.

A fishing boat off course might be an accidental visitor. But a Zodiac—it made no sense that a Zodiac or any sort of motorized raft would have been traveling the Gulf of Mexico on a pleasure cruise. More likely, it had been a landing boat from a larger craft, like the Hatteras or something even larger.

He'd retrieved his binoculars from the *Lorelei* before he started his island circuit and lifted them now toward the Gulf of Mexico stretching in turquoise splendor as far as the eye could see. There were shrimp boats out on the water, even the occasional sailboat. And fishing boats, of course.

Any one of the larger fishing craft could have carried the intruder boat, he recognized with frustration. Could someone in a boat have used a rubber dinghy to attempt an island landing, not realizing the place was inhabited?

He turned around and looked toward the house from where he stood by the furrowed sand. Stafford House's facade was clearly visible even from here, and would have been even more visible from the water.

Nobody could have mistaken Nightshade Island as deserted.

Movement on the second-floor veranda caught his eye. Shannon Cooper stepped out onto the balcony, joined by Lydia. Stepping behind the shelter of a scrubby sea oats stand, Gideon raised his binoculars for a closer, more covert look.

Shannon's straight, dark hair lifted in the breeze coming off the Gulf, fluttering around her heart-shaped face. Wind flattened her blouse against her body, revealing the shape of her small, round breasts and narrow waist.

Fire licking at his belly, he lowered the binoculars with a grumble of frustration. He'd been isolated on the island too long.

He resumed his walk around the island, trying to think who might want to sneak onto Nightshade Island and for what purpose.

But in the back of his mind, Shannon Cooper still leaned against the railing of the second-floor veranda, her hair floating in the breeze and her dark eyes full of mysteries.

Chapter Three

Gathering clouds hastened twilight, plunging the island into shadows soon after 5:00 p.m. Lydia had insisted Shannon rest before dinner, so she'd gladly taken the chance to shower off the heat of the day and change into fresh clothes.

"No need for formality around here, dear," Lydia had said with a smile. "We live on an island. Who's to care if we look a bit shabby?"

When Shannon ventured downstairs at six, she found Gideon alone in the kitchen, slicing onions. He glanced at her as she perched on one of the breakfast bar stools. "Settled in?"

"Yes, thank you." She tried to discern what he was preparing from the ingredients—sliced onions, red bell peppers and pieces of corn. "Stir fry?"

"Crab boil," he corrected.

"Where are the crabs?"

He slanted another look at her. "That's your job. There's a bucket outside and you can see the beach from here—"

"Don't let him tease you, Shannon." Lydia entered through the nearest French door, carrying a handful of zinnia cuttings. She arranged the colorful flowers in a clear vase and filled the bottom with water. "The crabs and shrimp are in the cooler. A nice man delivered them to us this morning." She set the flowers in the middle of the small dining table just beyond the kitchen. "Aren't these lovely?"

"Beautiful," Shannon agreed. "I caught a glimpse of the garden from my window. It's amazing."

Lydia smiled with pleasure as she washed her hands. "My husband loved to garden, so we made a habit of bringing in soil to fill the raised beds every spring." She looked with sad fondness at Gideon. "Dear Gideon helped me this year. It makes me a little weepy, I confess, to think that I won't be tending the garden next year."

"You'll be able to have a garden where you're moving, won't you?" Shannon asked.

Lydia retrieved a large pot from one of the lower cabinets and set it on the counter next to Gideon. "Yes. My sister-in-law tells me the backyard of my bungalow is perfect for gardening." She sighed. "It won't be the same, but I imagine it will be lovely anyway." She went back into the garden again.

"I made her sad," Shannon said with regret.

"Everything makes her sad these days," Gideon said shortly.

"Can I help you with anything?"

"Well," he said quietly, "how about we start with what you're really doing here?"

His question caught her off guard. "What?"

"I did some checking into Cooper Security. You're not the kind of outfit that hires out to help a rich widow pack up her house."

"What I'm here to do is a little more complicated than that."

He shot her a skeptical look. "Three months ago, Cooper Security helped put a high-ranking State Department official back in jail. And now I'm supposed to believe you're just here to archive General Ross's papers and collections? Really?"

"We do a lot of different kinds of jobs at Cooper Security," she protested.

Lydia returned to the kitchen, carrying a large bucket of blue crabs and jumbo Gulf shrimp. "Hope you're not allergic, Shannon. I suppose I should have asked before I planned the dinner tonight."

"Not allergic," she assured her hostess. "And my stomach is growling already!"

Within an hour, the pile of vegetables and seafood on the counter had transformed into a rustic dinner for three. It was messy and delicious, and by the time she helped clear the remains of their meal from the table, Shannon was stuffed and getting sleepy.

"I believe I'm going to call it a night, my dears," Lydia announced a little later, as the clock crept toward eight-thirty. "I have a Dick Francis novel waiting for me. He's left the hero in quite a pickle, and we must get him safely out." She waved her hand as Shannon showed signs of following her up the steps. "No need to retire at such an ungodly early hour. Stay and enjoy yourself. Poor Gideon must make do with just my company so much of the time. I'm sure he'd enjoy having someone new to talk to."

Lydia disappeared upstairs, apparently oblivious to the two wary, suspicious people she left staring at each other across the kitchen table.

"You don't have to stay," she said after a moment of uncomfortable silence.

"You want me to leave?"

His scrutiny set her nerves on edge, but she wasn't about to admit her unease to him. "Not if you don't want to."

He walked over to the counter. "Coffee?"

"No, thanks." Her earlier sleepiness had fled once Lydia left her alone with Gideon. The last thing her jangling nerves needed was more stimulation.

He returned from the kitchen empty-handed and waved toward the sofa in the front room. "Shall we?"

She wished he would smile. She'd liked the way he looked when he smiled, liked the surprising dimples and the humorous gleam in his blue eyes. Much more tempting, yes, but much easier on her nervous system.

But when he sat across from her perch on the sofa, pulling the large armchair closer, she felt as if she'd just taken a seat in the witness box.

"I don't know what you've heard about Lydia Ross or the general. Or me," he added with a quirk of his eyebrows. "But Mrs. Ross and I aren't looking to get in the middle of anything your outfit may be investigating. So if there's some hidden agenda here, pack your things and I'll take you back to the mainland first thing in the morning."

She bristled at his tone. "I am here to help Mrs. Ross. Period. I don't have any agenda other than that." She cocked her head. "Considering it was your boat that was sabotaged and your island that was breached by intruders, I'd say you're the one with an issue, not me."

Irritation lined his eyes. "Fair enough."

"I'm tired. I'm going to bed." She stood. "Good night."

He stood, unfolding himself to his full height, forcing her to look up. "Good night, Ms. Cooper."

She climbed the stairs to her second-floor bedroom. Shutting herself in the happy blue room, she sat on the springy mattress and stared at her reflection in the mirror. Her cheeks were flushed with annoyance and her dark eyes snapped with anger.

But at whom was she really angry?

She'd told Gideon she had no hidden agenda, but the truth was, she'd been wondering ever since Jesse gave her the assignment what his interest in Lydia Ross could be. Gideon was right; Cooper Security didn't handle personal archive security cases as a rule. Big companies with art or other collections that needed high security, maybe. But Jesse normally assigned his best-trained operatives to such cases, well aware that the valuables might be of interest to people willing to break dozens of laws to get their hands on them. General Ross's collection didn't seem to be anywhere near so valuable.

In fact, as Lydia Ross had explained during dinner, what most needed to be readied for safe transport were the general's private papers. Because of his high position in the U.S. Army at the time of his retirement, West Point and other institutions had expressed interest in housing some of the collection. Lydia had hired Cooper Security to help her sort through the papers to see if any needed extra preservation steps taken.

In that sense, Jesse had made a good choice in sending Shannon. She'd had special training in archival preservation, plus a master's degree in library science. She'd ended up primarily using her computer science degree in her work at Cooper Security, but she was capable of giving Lydia Ross good advice about preserving and cataloging her husband's work.

The last of daylight seeped away, shadows swallowing her room. And still she didn't move, either to dress for bed or turn on her light.

If there's some hidden agenda here...

She opened her cell phone, relieved to find a decent signal, and placed a call home.

Jesse answered on the first ring. "You're just now getting to the island?"

"No," she said, kicking herself. Jesse had told her to call when she reached the island, but in the confusion of the boat trouble and the island intruders, she hadn't given her brother a second thought. "We just had a crazy afternoon."

"Something happen?"

Normally, she'd be tempted to keep the drama of the afternoon to herself, knowing her brother's tendency to worry too much about her safety. But Gideon's suspicion had sparked a few questions of her own. "Actually, we had a little excitement today," she said aloud, telling him about the fuel tank sabotage and the arrival of unwelcome visitors to the island.

"Really." Jesse sounded more interested than surprised.

"You knew there would be trouble," she accused.

"I didn't know it. Not for certain."

"What am I really doing here, Jesse?"

"Exactly the job I gave you," he said sternly. "You help Mrs. Ross with the papers and her husband's collections. You keep your nose to the grindstone and stay out of trouble."

"That's it? You really think that's going to appease me?"

"Call me if anything else happens out of the ordinary. And get some sleep. You've had a long day." Jesse hung up before she could protest his paternal condescension.

She growled as she hung up the phone. Jesse wasn't the only one of her brothers and sisters who treated her as if she were still a child, but he was definitely the worst.

It wasn't her fault she was born last of the six. It wasn't her fault their mother had decided her career had to come before motherhood or marriage. She hadn't asked her siblings to make her their pampered, protected little pet.

She pushed herself off the bed and crossed to the window. It had rained a little during dinner, enough that the window sparkled with tiny diamonds of raindrops clinging to the glass. Moonlight peeked from behind thinning clouds, casting a cool blue glow across the night scene.

Through the blur of water, the thick stands of trees east of the house looked like a dark watercolor painting, all soft edges and mysterious shadows, punctuated here and there by the glow of lightning bugs flitting between the trees. It took a few seconds to realize that the light came not from flying bugs but from someone moving through the trees about two hundred yards away from the house.

Curious, she went out onto the balcony for a closer look. It was definitely a light, moving slowly through the trees. Was it Gideon doing another tour of the island for the night?

One way to find out, she thought, heading for the stairs.

When she reached the main floor, it was dark. Gideon was

no longer inside Stafford House, so the light in the woods must have been him.

She started to turn back toward the stairs when a niggling sensation at the back of her neck made her reverse course. She went instead to the side veranda that looked out across the trees to the east, hoping for a better view of the light she'd seen from her bedroom window. She had to unlock the dead bolt to step out onto the veranda. The door creaked as she opened it, the loud sound setting her nerves on edge.

Wincing, she eased out onto the wooden porch, wondering if the sounds she was making were loud enough to wake Lydia in her upstairs suite. She stepped gingerly toward the railing, trying to make as little noise as possible from here on.

A damp breeze blew in from the Gulf of Mexico, lifting her hair away from her face. Wishing she'd put her hair in a ponytail before she came downstairs, she finger-combed her hair out of her eyes to keep the swirling strands from blocking her view of the trees.

She stared for a long time, straining for any sign of the lights she'd seen earlier, but the woods were dark and quiet. She released a soft breath and started to turn back to the house when she spotted it.

A light, swinging back and forth with a rocking rhythm, as if held by someone moving slowly, steadily through the woods.

Was it Gideon?

She wasn't so sure anymore.

She moved around the veranda slowly until she was facing the back garden, where just beyond, a single-story house on stilts rose over the garden, perched on the highest point of land on the island. Like the Rosses' house, Gideon's residence also had a widow's walk around the top gable, though when Shannon had first spotted the house earlier during Lydia's guided tour of the house and gardens, she'd noticed the widow's walk on the caretaker's house looked new, as if it were a recent addition.

There were no lights on in the caretaker's house. No sign of movement inside. Maybe her first guess had been right. Maybe Gideon was taking a quick tour around the island to make sure everything was safe and secure for the night.

She returned to the door she'd left open, stopping just long enough to take another quick look at the woods.

Her heart skipped a beat. For there wasn't just one light flitting around through the woods anymore.

There were three.

If Gideon was out there somewhere in the dark, he wasn't alone. But was he in danger himself? Or was he collaborating with someone to do harm to Lydia Ross?

Shannon slipped back into the house, her heart racing, and tried to figure out what to do next. Gideon Stone might be surly and unpleasant, but he seemed to aim his bad attitude primarily at her. To Lydia, he seemed genuinely affectionate, and clearly Lydia returned the feelings. In lieu of evidence to the contrary, she decided to give Gideon the benefit of the doubt.

The question was, did he know there were people out there? And if not, what should she do, go bang on his door until he answered?

It was as good a plan as any, she decided, heading back around the house to the garden. A gravel path wound through the garden, past brightly colored coleus and merry daisies, beyond a small stone basin of water where, Lydia had told her earlier, birds regularly gathered for communal baths during the oppressive heat of summer afternoons.

At the end of the garden, the path to the caretaker's house went from neat gravel to an uneven walkway crowded on either side by scrubby grass that grew halfheartedly in the sandy soil. She stumbled a few times before she made it to the front porch. Seeing no sign of a doorbell, she rapped loudly on the door, grimacing as the sound echoed in the night.

There was no answer. Shannon knocked again, with no better result.

"Come on, Gideon!" she growled softly at the unyielding door.

But he didn't come.

Her pulse thundering in her ears, she hurried back along the crooked path, retracing her steps through the garden and ending up back on the veranda again. She circled the house once more to the place she started.

How much time had she just wasted trying to fetch Gideon? How much farther had the lights in the trees encroached?

She stayed in the shadows of the eaves, peering through the darkness until she spotted the lights again. They were stationary for the moment, glowing through the trees, flickering only when the breeze made the low-lying palmetto bushes and high-growing sea grasses dance back and forth.

Whoever was out there had stopped moving toward the house.

She wished she had a pair of binoculars like the ones Gideon had used earlier in the day. She should have packed a pair for herself, but she hadn't been planning on trying to spot intruders at night when she packed for the trip.

Slowly, she eased backward until her spine flattened against the French doors. Like it or not, she had to rouse Lydia and let her know something was happening outside. She would, at the very least, know how to sound the horn on the lighthouse, and maybe the noise would drive their intruders away again.

She eased open the doors and slipped inside, turning for one last look at the woods. Only the faintest creak of the floor beneath her feet gave her any warning at all.

A hand clapped over her mouth. A hard-muscled arm

snaked around her stomach, pulling her flush with a hard, hot body.

She raised her foot to stamp on her captor's instep, Cooper Security training kicking in before she had time to think.

Her captor sidestepped quickly, and her foot slammed on the ground, making her ankle tingle with pain.

"Don't do it again," warned a voice like steel in her ear.

The arms loosened, and she jerked away, turning around to face her captor. "You scared the hell out of me," she whispered.

Gideon Stone's eyes glittered like blue diamonds in the low lights, but he wasn't looking at her anymore. He was gazing past her, toward the woods in the east, his expression hard.

"You see the lights?" she asked softly.

"I do."

"Do you think the intruders are back?"

He nodded.

"Pretty brazen," she murmured.

"How many lights did you see?"

"Just three."

"Can't be sure that's all that's out there, though," he said thoughtfully, turning his gaze away from the door long enough to look down at her. "What were you going to do if I hadn't grabbed you?"

"Get Lydia up and see if we could sound the foghorn again."

"Let's not do that yet," he said softly, curling his palm over her arm and easing her away from the doorway. His hand was big and warm, sending unexpected sensations rippling through her flesh. "You stay here. If I'm not back in fifteen minutes, sound the horn. The switch is located in the kitchen pantry, second shelf, at the back."

She nodded, too breathless to speak.

He locked the French doors again, then pulled his Walther from a hip holster and checked the clip with practiced ease.

He chambered a round and looked down at her. "Fifteen minutes."

He disappeared into the shadows, heading toward the back of the house. She heard the faint snick of the back door dead bolt turning and felt her way through the dark until she reached the French doors. She tried the locks until she found the one he'd left open. She locked it behind him and leaned against the door, her heart racing.

Pushing the stem of her watch, she lit up the face so she could see the hands. Nine thirty-eight. At nine fifty, if Gideon didn't come back, she would sound the lighthouse horn.

And meanwhile, she had a GLOCK and knew how to use it. She hurried up the steps to the top floor, feeling her way rather than risk turning on the lights and possibly alerting the intruders.

Retrieving her GLOCK from her duffel bag, she headed back into the hallway and collided with another warm body.

She leaped back, flattening to the wall, already tugging the GLOCK from the holster.

"Shannon?"

She sagged against the wall. "Mrs. Ross."

Shannon heard a soft click and a flashlight flickered to life, illuminating Lydia's kind face and revealing the lethal gleam of a rifle gripped in her free hand. "What's going on, dear?" The older woman's tone was as gentle as ever, but the thread of steel beneath her words made Shannon smile despite her own nervous tension.

She brought Lydia up to speed and checked her watch. "In six minutes, if Gideon's not back here, we're supposed to sound the horn."

Lydia nodded. "If the horn continues sounding for more than five minutes, Terrebonne Fire and Rescue knows to send a boat to check on us."

"Can they hear the sound from that far away?" Shannon had heard the horn well enough from the boat earlier that day, but the *Lorelei* had been a long way from the shore by that time.

"It can be heard all the way to Bayou La Batre on a clear day." Lydia nodded at the GLOCK. "Do you know how to use that?"

Shannon cocked her eyebrow at Lydia and nodded at the Remington. "Do you know how to use *that?*"

Lydia smiled. "Touché." She turned off the flashlight.

They went downstairs together, easing through the dim shadows to the French doors on the eastern side of the house. Shannon peered through the clear glass. "I don't see the lights anymore."

"How much longer?" Lydia asked.

Shannon checked her watch. "Two minutes."

"Do you see any sign of Gideon?"

"No. He went out through the garden door."

"Perhaps we should make our way to the foghorn switch." Lydia hooked her free hand in Shannon's elbow, guiding her toward the kitchen. Shannon heard a pantry door creak open and a soft tapping sound. A light mounted inside the pantry snapped on, illuminating cans, bottles, boxes and, at the back of the second shelf, as Gideon had promised, a simple electrical toggle switch.

Shannon checked her watch. The second hand passed twelve. "Now," she said, her stomach aching with tension.

Lydia flipped the switch. Shannon braced for the moan of the foghorn.

But nothing happened.

Chapter Four

Three years of Marine Special Operations missions in Afghanistan. Four more years of duty in Iraq, clearing Baath Party holdouts and al-Qaeda in Iraq fighters out of war-weary villages hungry for peace and stability. He'd done a final three years on super-secret reconnaissance missions in Kaziristan and almost paid with his life.

Gideon had seen his share of impossible missions and no-escape situations. Being surrounded by at least three unknown subjects wasn't the most terrifying situation he'd ever dealt with. Not by a long shot.

But if he had his choice, he'd rather be elsewhere.

Time ticked inexorably away as his quarry circled him in the thick stand of pines and hardwoods that grew in abundance in the center of the island. He didn't want to give away his position by lighting the dial of his watch to check the time, but he was certain most of the fifteen minutes he'd given Shannon to wait before acting had already passed.

What would the men moving through the trees around him do once the lighthouse foghorn sounded?

He hadn't gotten very close to the intruders before they extinguished their lights, making recon substantially more difficult. Whoever they were, they were damn good at moving quietly through the dark, making him wonder for a while if they were wearing night-vision goggles. He gave himself a mental kick for not having a pair of his own, although in his defense, he'd thought he'd left his night-combat days far behind him.

He spotted one of the intruders again, finally. Male, based on his shape and size. He was dressed in a long-sleeved black shirt, dark trousers, a black hood and a balaclava, as they all had been. He wasn't visibly armed, though Gideon couldn't be sure he wasn't packing a concealed weapon. No sign of night-vision goggles, he saw to his relief.

Time ticked, and still no horn. Surely fifteen minutes had passed.

The sound of movement nearby set his nerves on edge. He hunkered lower, sheltered by a fallen pine tree that had gone down during the last tropical storm of the previous season. The leaves were brown and prickly but offered acceptable shelter.

He spotted movement to his right. A second man glided through the trees in near silence. "It's done," the newcomer said in a flat, Midwestern accent that sounded strangely familiar. Gideon frowned, trying to remember where he'd heard that voice before.

"Good." The first man's voice was pitched a step or two lower, the authority in his voice unmistakable. He seemed to be the leader.

"There's still Stone to deal with," Midwest said. "And the women."

"An old lady and a little stick of a girl. Still decent odds."

Gideon arched his eyebrows at the man's description of Shannon Cooper, remembering the way her windblown clothes had hugged her tempting curves and delightful valleys.

A third man circled around, moving with more speed than stealth. Through the pine fronds sheltering his hiding place, Gideon saw the leader wheel around aggressively as he reached them. Even though the third man was the largest of the three by far, he took a faltering step back as the leader hissed his displeasure.

"Stupid idiot, what part of silent force don't you understand?"

"No sign of Stone," the big man said in a growling bass. "I thought you said he would be trouble."

"He will," the leader said. "He's already on guard, thanks to the misstep earlier," the leaders said. "If we give him more time to shore up his defenses, we may not get a second chance. He thought he won today. He thinks he has time."

"Arrogant son of a bitch," Midwest muttered.

Gideon frowned. That remark sounded personal.

The men moved forward toward the house, away from Gideon's hiding place. With their backs to him, he took a chance to check his watch. Five past ten, and still no horn.

Where was Shannon?

"GIDEON'S NOT GOING to be happy that I'm letting you wander out here while there are intruders about," Shannon whispered to Lydia as she followed the older woman through the high sea grass behind the caretaker's cottage.

"He asked you to sound the horn," Lydia said sensibly. "We need to find out why the switch didn't work. And because you don't know how the contraption works and I do…"

They'd already checked the electrical connection to the house and found that the circuit appeared to be intact. "The problem must be on the lighthouse end," Lydia had told her solemnly. "The lines between the lighthouse and here run underground," she added, showing Shannon where the cable ran down into the sandy soil. "We have to go to the lighthouse to see if someone has disabled the horn on that end."

Shannon hadn't protested Lydia's pronouncement at first, her mind on Gideon somewhere out in the woods, outnumbered at least three to one. But the farther they walked from the house, the more vulnerable she felt.

Gideon had told her to stay put, and while she wasn't the sort of woman who needed a man to make her decisions for her, she knew the odds were against a natural explanation for the switch malfunction. More likely, someone had sabotaged the switch at the lighthouse.

Would that someone be guarding his handiwork? Were they walking into a trap?

She kept her hand on the butt of her GLOCK as she walked through the sand, her calves beginning to ache from the extra exertion. Up ahead, Nightshade Island Lighthouse glowed as pale as alabaster in the blue moonlight peeking through scudding clouds overhead.

"There are two places where the connection could have been disrupted," Lydia whispered as they neared the base of the lighthouse. "Here, where it comes out of the building and goes through a circuit box. And then there's also a connection up in the lighthouse itself."

Using a small penlight Shannon had grabbed from her duffel bag, they examined the connector. "It looks all right," Shannon murmured.

"That leaves the direct connection to the horn at the top," Lydia said, gazing up at the tall lighthouse. "There's a spiral staircase inside that leads to the service room and then up to the lantern room at the top, where the beacon is located. The beacon no longer works, but Gideon had an electrician from the mainland rig the horn. It's located on the catwalk outside the service room." Bathed with moonlight, her face creased with regret. "I'm afraid I can't manage all those stairs with my arthritic knees. You'll have to check it."

"How will I know if it's connected?"

"I'm not sure, but I suspect if it's been tampered with, you'll know."

"You'll have to stand guard," Shannon said, hating the idea of leaving Lydia alone. "I'll be back as quickly as I can."

She opened the faded wood door of the lighthouse, her

nerves twitching as her footsteps on the stone floor echoed up the tall structure. With her penlight, she traced the curve of the spiral staircase. At the top, there seemed to be a large, enclosed platform. That must be the service room.

She started up the steps, keeping her gaze directed upward. The steps were rusted but seemed sound enough, though the creaks and groans of metal echoed through the stone tower as she climbed.

She was breathing hard and her legs were shaking by the time she reached the service room, although she suspected fear, more than exertion, was the source of her weakness. She leaned against the damp stone wall and flashed her penlight around, taking in the small space.

There was little left of whatever had been inside the service room when the place was a working lighthouse. A rickety table, missing one leg and lying in a lopsided heap against one wall, took up half the space. Fortunately, it didn't block the door that led out to the narrow catwalk circling the lighthouse. Light seeped in through a cracked and dirty window. From elsewhere—either the broken window or the narrow space beneath the door—a draft blew in, cool and fragrant with the sea.

Heart racing, Shannon opened the door and crept out onto the metal catwalk. With the Gulf of Mexico spreading around the island as far as the eye could see, she couldn't pretend she wasn't standing on a rusted metal platform thirty feet in the air. She'd never considered herself afraid of heights, but that perception was about to be tested.

The foghorns were a pair of long metal horns that jutted out from a flat platform about ten feet to Shannon's left. Walking closer to the horns, she saw that whatever mechanism created their sound was back in the service room after all. She started to head back inside but paused, reorienting herself until she faced east, toward the wooded part of the island where Gideon had disappeared.

Suddenly, the air split with the booming moan of the foghorn, the sound rattling the catwalk beneath her feet. Shannon stumbled to her hands and knees, the penlight bouncing off the metal slats of the catwalk and tumbling over the side. The whole lighthouse seemed to vibrate with the horn's basso profundo, as if the structure was about to collapse in on itself and sink into the sandy earth below.

Shannon crawled to the door of the service room, dizzy from the loud vibrations of the horn. It took a second, therefore, to realize what she was seeing in front of her.

The door to the service room, which she had most certainly left open when she went out onto the catwalk, was now closed.

THE FOGHORN'S PLAINTIVE moan finally filled the air, sending birds rising from their treetop perches and soaring into the air in a cloud of dark silhouettes against the moonlit sky.

Ahead of Gideon, the three men froze only a hundred yards from Stafford House. Gideon crouched low, keeping an eye on them from behind the cover of a palmetto bush. He squeezed himself into a tighter ball as the men started moving quickly toward him, away from the house.

"I thought you said it was handled," the leader spat at Midwest.

"It was!"

"If that horn doesn't stop in five minutes, there'll be a rescue crew from the mainland," the big man growled. "I talked to a guy at the marina this afternoon when we regrouped."

"We can't get back there and stop it in five minutes," Midwest complained.

"Then we need to abort," the leader said firmly. "Again."

They passed Gideon's hiding place, moving at a fast march through the woods. A fourth dark shape glided out of the woods to join them on the fast trek back to the shoreline. They weren't even trying for stealth now.

As they moved farther away from Gideon's hiding place,

he was torn between following and heading back to Stafford House to make sure Shannon and Mrs. Ross were okay.

He couldn't be sure there were only four men on the island. There could be a whole other intruder force holding Lydia and Shannon captive at this very moment.

He watched only long enough to see the four men pile into the Zodiac. The engine started with a low roar and then they were dark shapes moving across the moonlit Gulf.

With his heart in his throat, he started running toward the house.

GROPING TO HER feet, Shannon pressed herself flat against the stone wall of the lighthouse, covering her ears and squeezing her eyes shut against another rush of dizziness. She tried the handle of the service room door and discovered, to her profound relief, that it was unlocked.

She pushed it open and stumbled inside. The sound of the horns was still loud, but the stone walls muted it enough that her ears stopped ringing and her head quit spinning. She dropped her hands away from her ears and peered into the gloom of the service room, wishing she had the penlight back.

There was enough light from the moon outside, pouring through the service room door, to see the path to the spiral stairway. From there, she could hold on to the rail and feel her way down to the bottom.

She paused at the top of the staircase, looking back into the murky bowels of the small room. She had a strange sense, all of a sudden, that she wasn't alone.

"Hello?" she whispered. She couldn't hear herself over the low keening of the foghorn.

Her eyes strained to see into the deepest shadows of the small room, and for a second, she fancied she saw a hint of movement. Fight-or-flight instincts kicking in, she started down the spiral staircase with more speed than was probably wise. Nevertheless, she made it down to the bottom with only one terrifying stumble and burst out of the lighthouse at a fast clip.

Lydia was waiting for her, her hands over her ears. "You did it," she said, her voice barely audible over the sound of the horn.

"I didn't touch the horns," Shannon replied as they hurried back through the sea grass to the caretaker's house. "They just came on while I was on the catwalk—literally knocked me to my knees."

"Let's go inside." Lydia grabbed her hand and pulled her to the stairs leading up to a wooden deck at the back of the caretaker's house. The door was unlocked, offering no barrier to their entry.

"Better!" Lydia said with a sigh of relief, shutting the door, and much of the noise, behind them. "I wonder how the horn fixed itself?"

"Perhaps the connector up in the service room is loose, and wind blowing through the cracked window knocked it back into place?"

"Perhaps." Lydia shrugged, leading Shannon through the darkened house as if she had the entire layout memorized. Perhaps she did. The house had been in her family for years, no matter who lived in it now.

It was hard to make out much in the gloom. Shannon got the impression of large furniture in sparing doses, which seemed to fit what she knew of Gideon Stone. He needed big things because he was a big man, but he probably didn't care much for clutter taking up the remaining space.

"This house used to be my son's. He would live here on the rare occasions he was home on leave."

The son who had died saving Gideon Stone's life, Shannon thought, wondering how Gideon felt, living here in a place that had once belonged to his friend. "You must miss him terribly."

"We all do." Lydia's hand caught hers briefly. "We knew it

was a possibility—a soldier's family doesn't send their loved one to war without knowing the potential costs. But we never really believed it would happen to us. We couldn't let ourselves think about it, or we'd go insane."

Shannon had seen two brothers go off to war. Several of her cousins had served their country as well. She'd been fortunate not to lose any of them, although she'd mourned with her sister Megan after the death of Megan's husband, Vince, in what they'd thought at the time was a combat death.

Thoughts of Vince's death led her mind straight to Gideon, who was still out there in the woods somewhere, surrounded by at least three men whose motives for being on this island were suspect in the extreme. "Do you think we should go back to the house?" she asked Lydia. "If Gideon doesn't find us there, what will he think?"

"Nothing good," Lydia admitted. For the first time since the ordeal began, Lydia sounded like a woman in her late sixties. "I am almost afraid to hope he's survived unscathed," she said in a weak voice. "I'm afraid I have become more accustomed to loss these days than not."

Shannon put her arm around the older woman. "I don't know Gideon very well, but if there's one thing I'm pretty sure about, it's that he's a big, tough guy who knows how to take care of himself. They don't call marines Devil Dogs for nothing, right?"

Lydia managed a smile. "My husband was appalled that Ford—our son—joined the Marine Corps. Edward was a soldier, through and through. Only the army was good enough for him."

"One of my cousins was in the navy, and two of his younger brothers were marines. He thinks they're lower than pig snot." At Lydia's surprised laugh, Shannon chuckled a little herself. "Not that he really thinks that—Sam and Luke are both the best, and J.D. knows it. But families are like that, I guess. Got to keep everyone in the right pecking order."

"I wish we'd given Ford a brother or sister. Perhaps it would be easier—" Lydia stopped and shook her head. "I don't suppose anything would make it easier."

Shannon started to respond, but a faint scrape outside the door stopped her in mid-breath. She tugged Lydia behind her and pulled her GLOCK, edging her way forward.

There was no peephole in the front door, only a narrow pane of glass about five and a half feet above the ground, clearly placed there by a tall man, because she had to rise on tiptoes to see anything.

A large, shadowy figure climbed the last porch step and scooted out of sight, moving quickly and smoothly.

"Someone's outside," she whispered to Lydia.

"Is it Gideon?"

"I can't tell," she whispered back. "You need to find someplace to hide, Lydia."

"My Remington and I will stay right here," Lydia retorted. She cocked the rifle for emphasis, making Shannon grin in spite of the terror rising like bile in her throat.

A faint rattle of the door handle set her into motion. She slid sideways to flatten herself against the wall by the door.

Like all Cooper Security employees, including clerks and interns, Shannon had undergone rigorous self-defense and crisis management courses before she'd been allowed to work for the company. One of the things she'd been taught was how to disarm an armed intruder.

Considering how much her family babied her, Shannon had despaired of ever having reason to use that particular skill. But now that the opportunity was upon her, she was beginning to appreciate just what her family had been trying to protect her from.

Tension as thick as any she'd ever known. Rage at being forced to even think about drawing a weapon on a fellow human being. And the gnawing, sickening fear that she was going to have to pull the trigger and take someone's life.

But she had no time to dwell on any of those emotions, for the front door creaked open and the large figure pushed inside, immediately swinging his gun arm in a sweeping motion.

Shannon caught his arm as it swung toward her, bringing it downward with a sharp pull while she kept her body safely out of range. She banged her knee hard against the back of the intruder's knee, knocking him off balance. They both hit the floor in a tangle, the intruder landing atop her with a low groan, pinning her to the hard pine.

The intruder's left hand found her weapon hand, anchoring it in place against the floor before she could bring up the GLOCK. His right hand swept up her body, pausing for a moment at the curve of her breast, his touch firm and shockingly intimate. She tried to bring her knee up between his legs, but the intruder trapped her leg between his knees, blocking her ploy. His hand fell away from her breast.

Suddenly, light filled the room, so bright she had to squint against the painful contraction of her pupils. She peered up at her captor, her body going from hot to cold to hot again in a span of seconds, making her shiver.

"You're not much for staying put, are you?" Gideon asked, gazing back at her with amusement in his intensely blue eyes.

Chapter Five

"Are you certain you didn't touch anything in the service room that might have repaired the connection to the fog-horn?" Gideon asked from his lookout spot on the widow's walk. Lydia had gone to her bedroom to rest, although he doubted she'd be able to sleep much after all the excitement of the evening. But Shannon had insisted on staying with him on watch from his perch atop Stafford House.

Despite the continuing danger and his lack of a foolproof plan to combat it, Gideon's mind kept returning again and again to the feel of Shannon's firm, softly rounded breast against his palm. He had never had quite so much trouble focusing on an imminent threat before. He didn't like feeling out of control.

"I didn't touch anything. I barely walked into the service room before I went out on the catwalk," Shannon insisted. "I didn't know what I was looking for, and I thought the connector might be on the outside, where the horns are."

She stood at the opposite end of the front railing from him, her voice carrying lightly on the night breeze. She looked alert and businesslike, her GLOCK in its holster on her hip, the snap unfastened for easy retrieval. If she was tired from her earlier exertions, it didn't show. Must be nice, he thought wearily, to be young.

"That must have been loud, having it go off right by you."

"Scared the hell out of me," she admitted with a sheepish grin. "And going out on that catwalk already had me on edge. Literally."

He followed her troubled gaze to the lighthouse, not sure whether he should feel angry that she and his boss had ventured out into the night against his express orders or glad that she'd managed, however accidentally, to sound the alarm just in time.

"They knew the horn was a signal to Terrebonne Fire and Rescue," he murmured. "They've done their homework."

Shannon moved closer to him, wrapping her arms around herself as if she were cold. He clenched his fists on the balcony railing, quelling the urge to pull her close and warm her with the fire burning low in his own belly. "I'm sorry about earlier," he said.

Her eyes flickered up to meet his. "In your house?"

He nodded. "I wasn't sure who was attacking me in the dark."

Her lips curved slightly, her eyelids lowering until she was looking at him through a veil of dark lashes. "Same here."

"You did a good job," he added. "Taking me down."

She looked down at her hands where they gripped the rail next to his. "You pinned me, so I guess it wasn't that good a job."

"I was Marine Special Operations. There are few men in the world who could take me down hand to hand," he said flatly. "You did it well."

She looked up again. "Thanks. I learned from a marine."

"Your brother?"

She nodded. "Everyone who works for Cooper Security goes through training. Jesse thinks we should all be able to acquit ourselves in a way that brings honor to the company."

He could tell from the dry recitation that she was parroting her brother's words. "He has a point."

"I know." There was a plaintive tone to her voice. "He's just not very good at allowing people to use what they've learned."

"And by 'people,' you mean you?"

She smiled sheepishly again. "Megan—that's my sister—says he'd probably let me do more things if I didn't whine about it quite so much. Sorry for the pity party."

"I'll put in a good word for you if I ever talk to him." He couldn't quite hide his irritation.

Her gaze snapped up to his. "You don't trust us, do you?"

"It seems a small job for such a big company."

"We do small jobs," she said defensively.

He knew they did. After dinner, when Shannon had gone up to her room, he'd checked up on Cooper Security, via the internet and a couple of calls to old friends from the Corps. He'd learned quite a bit about the way the company did business. "Most of those small jobs are for people who can't pay for the services you offer. Pro bono. Lydia Ross is no charity case. Which makes me wonder exactly what your brother hopes to get out of this job besides the paycheck."

Shannon's eyes narrowed. "I don't know. Maybe Jesse knew General Ross personally or something."

Gideon considered the possibility. "Unless your brother was pretty high in the Marine Corps command, he wouldn't have had much contact with an army general," he said.

She shook her head. "He retired as a captain. Didn't mix much with the upper brass."

"And you didn't think it strange he sent you on this job?"

A self-conscious smile darted across her face. "I was just glad to get out from under a computer for once."

He arched an eyebrow at her comment.

"Along with my archival science degree, I have a computer science degree. I've been Cooper Security's head of Information Technology."

He grinned. "You're an IT geek?"

"You got it, big guy. Wanna see my pocket protector?" she asked with a waggle of her well-shaped black eyebrows.

She was damn cute, he thought, with her big brown eyes and infectious grin. About ten years too young for him, and eons too innocent. If he had any sense, he'd put those thoughts right out of his idiotic brain.

Right now, however, he seemed to have no sense at all, for despite the serious danger they had been in tonight—were still in, regardless of Terrebonne Harbor Patrol's promise to keep an eye out for any further incursions—he was overwhelmed by the urge to kiss her.

"What do they want from Lydia?" she asked, interrupting his thoughts.

"The general's archive," he said. It was the only thing that made sense.

Her brow furrowed. "You mean his collections?"

"I suppose those would be a robber's likeliest target," he admitted, although it wasn't what he'd meant. "The general owns some unique items—things he bought during overseas tours of duty, art he's collected over the years. Mrs. Ross owns things as well that must be quite valuable."

"But you said *his* archive, first," she noted, her gaze narrowed.

He sighed. Cute as a button and smart as a whip. "I suppose some of his writings have intrinsic historical value."

"Enough to warrant an armed invasion?"

"That's the question, isn't it?" He looked to the east, where he'd last seen the intruders as they piled aboard a Zodiac Bayrunner motorized raft with carefully controlled haste and skimmed across the waters of the Gulf of Mexico, heading directly south. They must have had a boat anchored out there somewhere, just beyond the sight horizon. He'd been tempted to hop aboard the *Lorelei* and chase them down, but he'd had Mrs. Ross and Shannon Cooper to think about.

Not to mention, after the sabotage this morning—yesterday

morning, he amended mentally, noting the first pinkish-gray lightening of the eastern sky—he couldn't be sure the *Lorelei* was even seaworthy at the moment.

"We're not safe here," Shannon said quietly. "And short of ringing the island with armed guards—"

"Mrs. Ross will understand if you want to leave."

She rounded on him, her expression fierce. "And leave the two of you here to deal with this mess alone?"

He couldn't hold back a smile. "You and your pocket protector gonna keep us safe?"

Her chin jutted. "Don't forget my GLOCK."

He looked down at the sleek black pistol hugging her waist. "Don't forget you have an actual job to do here. Your company wasn't hired to provide security."

She cocked her head. "And from what I understand, you were hired to help the Rosses take care of the island," she noted. "Ferry them back and forth to the mainland, maintain the buildings and premises—"

Touché, he thought. "Mrs. Ross won't stand for private bodyguards. She had one growing up and loathed the sense of captivity."

Shannon's expression softened. "So you're most expressly *not* her bodyguard. You're just a caretaker with a Walther P99 and the general build of an Abrams tank."

He grinned at her description. "Exactly."

"Then I guess I'm an archivist with a GLOCK and outstanding self-defense skills." She smiled back at him, looking so damn adorable that his gut tightened with unwelcome longing.

He forced his gaze back to the eastern sky, nodding at the first rosy streak of daybreak. "Guess we made it through the night, more or less unscathed, huh?"

She followed his gaze and released a soft sigh. The cool morning breeze off the Gulf lifted her dark hair, sending a few strands dancing against his cheeks. She smelled like a fresh morning rain, despite having traipsed through the sea grass, climbed up and down a thirty-foot lighthouse and taken down a special forces marine twice her size with her bare hands.

She was formidable, he thought, rolling the word around in his head, savoring it.

Fearing it.

He'd known the second he saw her waiting on the pier at Terrebonne Marina that she was going to be trouble for him.

He just hadn't realized how much.

"Go get some sleep," he told her.

"I'm fine," she said with a shake of her head.

"I'm going to need you awake later today when I have to crash," he said firmly. "Get a few hours of sleep and then you can be on guard duty. Besides, don't you have an actual job to do here? You need to be rested or you'll fall asleep over all those papers."

She eyed him suspiciously, as if she suspected him of making up an excuse to get her to do what he wanted. And maybe he was in a way. He certainly wanted her to take her sweet smile and bright brown eyes and leave him in peace, if only for a little while.

But he meant what he said about spelling him. Even when he'd been on active duty in war zones, where sleep had been a precious commodity, he'd taken advantage of any chance to rest.

He was fortunate that Shannon Cooper was here, armed and apparently trained to anticipate and deal with danger. The timing of her arrival couldn't have been better in that one way.

And if having her around created other, unexpected problems for him, he was a big boy. He'd learn how to deal.

SHANNON HADN'T EXPECTED to fall straight to sleep, but she'd barely stripped off her clothes and slid beneath the covers of her bed before she was asleep and dreaming.

Dreaming of the lighthouse.

In her dream, all was dark. Fog rolled in, dense and chilling. Fingers of moisture writhed across her flesh, sending shivers tumbling through her. She stood on the catwalk, her back to the open doorway of the service room. The foghorn moaned a low warning of impending danger, rattling the metal mesh of the catwalk beneath her feet.

She felt more than heard movement behind her. Slowly, she turned around, the motion sluggish, heavy with dread.

The doorway to the service room was a gaping maw, a gaze into the belly of a cold and ruthless beast. Even as the catwalk shimmied beneath her, a stark reminder of her precarious position, the very idea of entering the service room filled her with abject fear.

Something—someone—was inside the room, waiting. And there was no way to escape, no way to get away from the lighthouse but through that black and waiting doorway.

A shrill bell clanged, making her jump. The catwalk shifted beneath her feet, dropping precipitously. She leaped forward, into the blackness, no options left.

The bell echoed in her head as she groped her way through the darkness, seeking out the tiny pinpoint of light that glittered, miles and miles distant. If she could make it to that light—

With a flash, the darkness became molten daylight, pouring across her face and warming her skin. Shannon opened her eyes to the blue room at the top of Stafford House and the discordant clamor of her travel alarm.

She shut the alarm clock off, her heart still racing from the fast-vanishing remnants of her dream. Something about the lighthouse—

Once dressed, she headed downstairs and found Gideon sitting at the kitchen table, the Remington rifle propped against the counter beside him. He was cleaning the Walther, the pungent smell of gun oil filling the room. "I usually do this at the caretaker's cottage," he murmured as she approached. "Mrs. Ross doesn't like the smell in her kitchen. But I wanted to stick close to the first point of attack."

She pulled out a chair and sat across from him. "Is Mrs. Ross still asleep?" Lydia had not yet risen for the day when Shannon took Gideon's advice to get some sleep.

"She's up. She made some cheese croissants for breakfast if you'd like something to eat. They're still warming in the oven. There's milk and orange juice in the fridge."

She could smell the warm, buttery aroma of the croissants now, eclipsing even the tang of gun oil. "Would you like one?"

"I've already eaten, thanks."

She retrieved a flaky, cheesy bun and put it on one of the small stoneware plates sitting next to the stove. There were also a couple of clean tumblers sitting by the refrigerator; she grabbed one and poured a cup of milk as well.

She returned to the table with her breakfast, cocking her head to one side as Gideon looked up and viewed her approach with a thoughtful look.

"What?" she asked as she sat across from him once more.

"Milk," he said, his lips curving slightly.

"Yes, it is," she said carefully, feeling as if she were the butt of a joke she couldn't understand.

"Wholesome choice." Dimples formed in his cheeks, even as he was trying not to smile.

Now she knew she was the butt of a joke. "Clearly, you find something about that funny."

"How old are you, twenty-two? Twenty-three?"

"Twenty-six," she answered, beginning to see where his thoughts had gone. "Yes, I'm young. Is there something wrong with that?"

He shook his head. "Not a thing."

"You're not exactly old," she muttered, picking at the edge of the cheese croissant.

"I'm thirty-four."

"Oh." She slapped her hand across her chest, feigning shock. "Sorry, I was wrong. You're ancient."

"It's not just your age," he said with a gentleness that did more to irritate than soothe her. "You have this look about you that tells me you were sheltered most of your life. You're the baby of the family, right? Older brothers and sisters who protected you, tried to keep you from experiencing the bad things in life. Parents who doted on you, adored you—"

"Parent," she corrected flatly. "I had a father who doted on me. My mother left when I was practically a baby. Didn't want to be a mother or a live-in wife, so she went to follow her own dreams."

He winced. "Sorry."

She shrugged. "I barely knew her anyway. She drops by now and then with nice presents. Could be worse."

"My dad killed my mom when I was fifteen," he said grimly.

And that would be worse, she thought. "I'm sorry."

He acknowledged her sympathy with a nod. "My point is—"

"Your point is that you've decided I should go home so you don't have two helpless women to protect instead of just one."

"My point is, no matter how prepared you might think you are to handle whatever it is that's happening here, you're probably not. Those were seriously bad guys. I'm pretty sure they were armed and ready to do bodily harm if challenged."

"They must know who you are, or at least what you are," she pointed out. "They tried to keep you out of the game by sabotaging the *Lorelei*'s engine. You'd pose a pretty big challenge to whatever they came here to do."

"But when it didn't work, they came back anyway. Ready to take the chance of dealing with me."

"Did the harbor patrol find anything out there last night?" Gideon had told her about the military-style raft and his theory about a boat anchored farther offshore.

"Nothing," he answered, "but by the time they got here and got the story about what was going on, the other boat could have been halfway to Waveland, Mississippi, for all we know."

"I don't think they're taking off from that far away," she said thoughtfully. "And they do seem to be working on the premise that they'd rather not deal with you if they can arrange things that way."

He didn't look convinced. "They didn't have any problem dealing with me last night. They came ready for a fight."

"But they apparently sneaked here night before last and tampered with the boat, right? They would have preferred to keep you completely out of the mix." She looked across the table, took in his broad shoulders, powerful arms and hard-jawed look of determination, and understood that preference completely. "They'd rather deal with a frail old lady—"

Gideon snorted, making her smile.

"Well, what they think is a frail old lady," she amended.

"Glad you clarified," Lydia said drily, entering the kitchen carrying a large plastic container in which she'd placed a couple of smaller cardboard boxes. Gideon, finished with his reassembly of the Walther, laid the pistol on the table and rose to unburden her.

She thanked him and sat in the chair by Shannon. "I've brought you some of the general's letters," she said. "And one of the boxes your brother requested I purchase for transporting Edward's papers."

"It's perfect," she said with a smile. "But I'd have been happy to do the work in the general's study."

Lydia exchanged a look with Gideon, who picked up the Walther's magazine from where it lay on the table and slid it into the chamber.

"What am I missing?" Shannon asked.

"Apparently nothing," Gideon murmured. Sliding the Walther into a compact holster, he stood to clip the holster to his jeans and grabbed the cotton button-up shirt hanging on the back of his chair. He shrugged it on over his T-shirt to hide the pistol from view and rolled up the sleeves.

"Gideon is taking the *Lorelei* and heading back to the mainland for a few hours," Lydia said. "To get the fuel system serviced."

"By yourself?" Shannon looked up at him, an uneasy feeling curling in the middle of her gut.

"You're worried about being here alone?" he asked.

"No," she answered, although she was, a little. But her greater concern was his going to town alone. He was the obvious target for the men who'd invaded the island the night before. If they could find a way to take him out, getting past what resistance Shannon and Lydia could offer would be that much easier.

He was in far graver danger at the moment than she or Lydia.

"I've called a few friends of mine in the area who have fishing charters. They're going to bring their clients fishing off the island today."

She couldn't hold back an admiring smile. "Is the fishing good off the island?"

"Good enough." He flashed his dimples at her. "You should be okay with so many boats out on the water around the island today. I'll try not to be long." He started toward the front door.

Shannon followed him out to the porch. "Where are you really going?"

"I'm just going to take a look around. Ask some questions."

"Have you checked the boat to make sure it's even minimally seaworthy?"

He gave her a pointed look. "Of course."

"What if they placed a bomb under the keel?"

"I checked that out, too, while you were sleeping." He grimaced and started down the porch steps. "Believe it or not, I do know what I'm doing most of the time."

Feeling like an idiot, she trotted down the stairs after him. He turned at the foot of the steps, giving her a quizzical look.

"Be careful," she said, unable to think of anything she could say that would change his mind.

"I will. You take care, too." He bent his head toward her, and for a crazy moment, she thought he was going to kiss her. But he just lowered his voice and added, "Take care of Mrs. Ross. She's tougher than she looks, but not nearly as tough as she thinks."

Then, before she could blink, he'd turned and gone, heading down the path to the boathouse.

She watched him go, listening with worry to the sound of the engine as he backed the *Lorelei* out of the boathouse and turned it around, heading into open water. Long after the Hatteras Convertible was out of sight, she stayed where she stood and watched the water with a sick feeling in the pit of her stomach, unable to shake the feeling that he was heading straight into the heart of danger with no one to watch his back.

Chapter Six

Terrebonne Marina, despite the name, was not Terrebonne's primary marina. That honor belonged to Bay Pointe, an eighty-slip marina on the western shore of Terrebonne Bay. Most of the larger yachts and pleasure craft preferred Bay Pointe's upscale accommodations, but Gideon had convinced General Ross to stick to the smaller, family-run marina on the eastern shore, appealing to the old soldier's inculcated suspicion of strangers.

Even before this most recent invasion, there had always been danger involved in living in such an isolated, unprotected place. Drug runners, pirates, even the possibility of terrorists seeking a less difficult point of entry to the United States for their destructive schemes—all theoretically posed potential peril for the Rosses and Nightshade Island.

At Terrebonne Marina, at least, Gideon knew all his fellow slip mates by name and their boats by sight. Wandering around Bay Pointe to find a boat he'd never seen, his only clue the fact that somewhere on board there'd be a Zodiac Bayrunner, was one of his less inspired ideas.

The marina office receptionist had been little help. "Many of the larger vessels have lifeboats," she'd told him with a harried air, clearly up to her elbows in paperwork. "If your friends are here, maybe you could just look around and see if you spot them."

He didn't bother explaining that the only time he'd seen his "friends," they'd been wearing black masks and sneaking around a private island, clearly intending to commit a crime.

But he thought he might recognize the Bayrunner again. For one thing, thanks to its larger size, it wasn't likely to be the preferred choice of inflatable for the average yachter. And he'd noticed a bright green patch on the rear of the port buoyancy tube. All he had to do was visit every one of the Bay Pointe slips to see if any of the boats had that Bayrunner on board.

His lack of sleep was starting to catch up with him, aided by the August heat and humidity. By ten-fifteen, he'd begun to regret bringing his Walther along, as its presence prevented him from shedding the extra shirt he'd worn to cover his holster.

He stopped halfway down the pier at a small waterside bistro and ordered the least appalling iced coffee choice they offered. The barista, a lean, tanned blonde woman in her early thirties, handed over the iced coffee with a flirtatious smile. "New to Bay Pointe?" she asked.

"Something like that," he answered, dispensing with the straw and gulping down the coffee, willing the caffeine to do its job.

"Which boat is yours?" she asked curiously, wiping the already clean bar in front of him.

"The one with the huge black Zodiac Bayrunner hanging from the back davits," he answered wryly.

"Nice yacht," she said with approval.

His gaze snapped up to hers. Her eyes widened and she took a half step back from him, as if she saw something in his face that scared her.

He forced his expression back to neutral friendliness. "Yeah? What do you think of the color? Too much?"

She relaxed a little, shrugging. "Blue and white is a pretty standard color pattern, isn't it?" She smiled at him, the flirtatiousness back. "One time, some guy rented a slip for the winter with the most hellacious yellow-and-orange Viking—" She shuddered dramatically. "You made a good choice with the Azimut. Though don't you think that Bayrunner's a little big? Should have opted for one of the smaller RIBs, maybe a Zoom."

"You know your watercraft," he said with a smile, noting her use of RIB, the acronym for rigid inflatable boat.

"My ex used to be a boat pilot for hire." She grimaced. "Until he ran off to Barbados with some rich guy's daughter."

"Sorry to hear that."

She flashed him a smile. "Better off without him. You going to be docked here long?"

"Remains to be seen," he said vaguely. "I'd better shove off. Thanks for the coffee." He pulled out his billfold and started to place a five on the counter before he realized he was playing the role of a yacht owner. He made it a twenty. "And the conversation."

He could tell she'd like to extend the conversation, but he didn't have the time nor, to his surprise, the inclination. His thoughts were occupied already by the women he'd left behind him, unguarded, on Nightshade Island.

He walked out of the open-air bistro and headed to his right, thinking about everything the young bartender had told him about the Azimut. Blue and white—standard color pattern, she'd called it, which meant it was probably mostly white with blue trim work or detailing.

Behind him, the barista called out, "Did you get turned around? Your slip's back that way."

He turned to look at her, pasting on what he hoped looked like a sheepish smile. "New marina," he said with apology and reversed course, heading back toward the southern end of the marina.

He passed the entry pier, where he'd been already, and started looking for an Azimut. He could hardly have asked her for size specifications, but he imagined it would have to be fairly large for the barista to call it a nice yacht. Eighty-feet long or larger.

He spotted a likely prospect in one of the outer slips. Tugging his baseball cap lower over his eyes, he walked unhurriedly down the pier toward the yacht. It was a ninety-footer, probably twenty years old but still in good shape. White with navy trim and, more to the point, a Zodiac Bayrunner suspended from davits at the back of the boat.

Walking past the blue-and-white motor yacht slowly, he searched for signs of occupancy without being obvious about it. He saw no one on deck, but there was a lot of yacht not visible from the outside.

He glanced idly at the back of the boat. Plain blue letters spelled out *Ahab's Folly,* and beneath that in smaller letters, *Galveston, Texas.* The letters all looked new, as if the boat's name had been recently changed.

There was a green patch on the Zodiac's port buoyancy tube. He tamped down a smile of triumph.

If there was anything he knew how to do, it was reconnaissance. And sometimes, that meant hunkering down for a while and just watching to see what developed. Three slips down, there was another small pier-side shop, this one a video arcade with an attached soft drink bar. He entered, noting there were almost no teenagers inside, as there would have been when he was a kid. Kids today all had smartphones with the games built in. Instead, most of the dozen or so game players thumbing the buttons on the video games were men and a few women in their late twenties and early thirties, reliving their youth with each digital explosion and high-pitched beep and chirp.

Gideon stopped at the bar and bought lemonade from the bored counter clerk. He didn't bother to try to worm information out of the kid, who looked as if he'd prefer to be anywhere but the arcade. It wasn't likely the boy had looked up from his own smartphone long enough to notice any comings or goings around the Azimut.

There was a bench just outside the video arcade, sheltered from the late-morning sun by a large red awning. Gideon settled on the bench, sipped his lemonade and pulled his cell phone from his pocket, dialing the Stafford House landline. Lydia Ross answered on the second ring.

"I thought I should check in," he said, not wanting to get her hopes up or worry her further. "Is Shannon around?"

"Of course." There was a smile in Mrs. Ross's voice. Seconds later, Shannon came on the phone.

"Still alive?" she asked in a dry drawl that made him smile.

"So far," he answered. "I think I've found the Zodiac. And the boat it rode in on. But don't let on to Mrs. Ross. I don't want her to worry about me while I'm figuring out what to do."

"Okay," she said slowly. "What options are on the table?"

"Well, for now, I'm doing a little surveillance. Probably going to be doing that awhile, so I don't want y'all to worry."

"Easier said than done."

"I really do know what I'm doing," he assured her.

"Okay."

"You making any headway with the archiving?"

"Just opened a big box of things that look intriguing," she answered, real excitement in her voice. "Tons of history, right at my fingertips. I know it sounds silly, but it's like—"

"Like hitting a moving target at five-hundred yards in bad weather?" he asked with a smile.

"I suppose so," she replied, laughter in her voice. But the amusement faded quickly. "Be careful. Check in often so Lydia doesn't worry."

He wondered if she was worried, too. She'd seemed anxious when she walked him out that morning, and when he'd looked back toward the island as the Hatteras cut through the Gulf water, she'd still been standing there, watching him drive away.

Movement on the deck of *Ahab's Folly* drew his attention back to the issue at hand. "I've got to go."

"What's happening?"

"I'll call back soon," he promised and shut off the phone.

A tall, muscular man in his late twenties came out on the deck of the Azimut and started washing down the suspended Bayrunner, his movements oddly violent for such a mundane task. Judging by the man's size and exaggerated body movements, he must have been the big guy who'd crashed through the woods last night, earning the censure of his leader.

One down, three to go.

DESPITE THE CARDBOARD box full of letters, papers and journals sitting in front of her like a treasure trove of history, Shannon's thoughts kept wandering across the bay to Terrebonne and Gideon Stone's "surveillance," as he'd termed it. She couldn't help wondering—and worrying—about how easily he could be recognized. He was a big man, a distinctive man. After less than a day of knowing him, she was pretty sure she could have spotted him in any crowd.

What made him think the men who'd invaded the island, men who clearly knew enough about him to have tried to avoid storming the island while he was around, wouldn't recognize him as well?

Focus, Shannon.

She picked up one of the journals, a thick, pocket-size notebook with a hard cover. Inside, instead of the daily diary of activities she'd expected, she found a series of letters that clearly formed words, but no language she'd ever seen before.

Lydia was in the kitchen, elbow deep in chopped lettuce for the Greek salad she was preparing for lunch. Shannon hesitated interrupting her in a task that seemed to give her a great deal of contentment, but her curiosity overcame her reluctance.

She carried the journal to the kitchen. "Lydia, have you ever seen anything like this before?"

Lydia set down her chopping knife and looked at the journal, her brow furrowed. "Quite unreadable, isn't it?" she asked, sounding puzzled.

"Could it be another language?"

"Edward was fluent in many, as am I, but this is no language I've ever come across," Lydia said firmly. "Perhaps it's code."

Shannon had guessed as much. "Did your husband deal in code very often? Maybe in his work?"

"There was a lot about his work that he couldn't tell me." Lydia looked apologetic. "Anything to do with any mission was off limits until afterward, and much remained off limits entirely."

"Preserving mission integrity."

Lydia smiled. "Loose lips sink ships."

"Do you mind if I take a crack at this later? I took a code-breaking class in college and who knows?" She waggled her eyebrows at Lydia. "Maybe I'll discover a state secret."

"Just don't tell me," Lydia laughed.

"Because then I'd have to kill you?"

"Exactly!" With a smile, Lydia turned back to her salad making. "Did Gideon say whether he'd be back for lunch?"

"I believe he plans to grab a bite on the mainland," Shannon replied, crossing back to the low coffee table where she'd left the box of papers. "Why don't we have lunch out on the front veranda? It's not too hot in the shade, and you really can't beat the view."

Lydia readily agreed, and they ended up outside an hour later, enjoying the salad Lydia had prepared and talking about their ordeal the night before.

"I'm tempted to go back to the lighthouse, now that it's

daylight, and see if I can find the penlight I dropped," Shannon said. The ground beneath the lighthouse was soft and sandy, so there was a chance that the light hadn't been damaged by the fall.

"I'm not sure it's a good idea to go out on your own with Gideon not here," Lydia protested. "Even in daylight. I'm afraid I won't feel safe until we know exactly what those men wanted last night."

"You don't think it could simply be your husband's memorabilia?"

Lydia shook her head. "The items Edward brought home are extremely valuable to me, and some may be historically valuable to some museum or even West Point, but they're not items one could easily sell on the black market. Or the open market, either."

"What about your own personal valuables?"

Lydia smiled. "Most of my money is here in this house, in this property. I was never one for diamonds or jewels." She showed Shannon a blue cameo locket on a gold chain around her neck. "Edward gave me this locket for our fortieth anniversary. He'd wanted to replace the engagement ring he'd given me when we were both young and starting out, but he saw this locket in an antique store and knew I'd love it, so he bought it instead. Less expensive than a diamond, but so much more valuable to me." Her eyes grew misty with memory. "My parents were appalled that I'd put my money on a young soldier from Wetumpka, but Edward was all I really wanted or needed."

Shannon wondered if her parents had felt that way at one time. Her mother, putting herself through college but falling for a man who was as married to the town he loved, the town he served as a sheriff's deputy, as he was to her. Such a bad choice for both of them, lives so radically different that it could never have worked.

And it hadn't.

"How did you know General Ross was the right one?" she asked.

Lydia laughed. "Every young woman your age I've ever met has asked that question. Did you know that?"

Shannon blushed, feeling like an idiot. "I'm sorry. Stupid question."

"Not stupid," Lydia disagreed. "Just universal. To tell you the truth, I don't know that I knew he was the right one until long after we were married. I think love is more than just the right set of circumstances. It's also about making good choices, choices with each other in mind instead of just yourself. When you're both making the right choices, ones that keep you together rather than drive you apart—that's a relationship that will last."

Her parents had made the wrong choices, she thought. Dug their heels in and refused to budge for each other. Megan swore their parents still really loved each other, and Shannon supposed her sister could be right. They'd never divorced, neither showing any desire to marry anyone else. Her parents did seem to enjoy each other's company when her mother came to town, and her mother usually stayed at the family home when she was there.

Megan seemed certain their parents still slept together when their mother Jean visited. Shannon hadn't screwed up the courage to ask her how she'd come to that conclusion.

Out in the Gulf, a fishing boat drew within a hundred yards of the shoreline. The boat's horn honked several times, some long, some short.

Lydia smiled. "Arthur Logan. Dear man. He drops by now and then and leaves us some lovely bonito and flounder for the freezer."

"You seem to know all the fishing guides," Shannon said. Every hour so far, one of the local fishermen had come by and sounded a signal, different each time. Lydia had explained they were signaling their initials in Morse code.

"All those fishermen know Morse code?" Shannon had asked.

"No, but I do," Lydia had explained, "and Gideon gave them the signals so I'd be reassured."

"Are you sure you don't want to pack up everything and head for the mainland tonight?" Shannon asked as she helped Lydia carry their lunch dishes back into the house. "We could take everything straight up to Cooper Security and sort it out there. We can put you up in a hotel—"

"I refuse to be run out of my house one minute earlier than I intended," Lydia said with conviction. "I do appreciate the offer, but I've already lost my husband and my son. I will not lose my dignity to a small group of larcenous thugs."

Shannon could appreciate Lydia's sentiment, even if she wasn't sure the woman was making a wise decision. Running away from trouble wasn't exactly a Cooper family trait, either.

She spent the rest of the afternoon going through two more boxes of the general's belongings, sorting out the mishmash of documents into separate boxes. Personal correspondence in one, official correspondence in another. The general's work-related writings in another still. She held out the coded journal to play around with later.

Gideon called once that afternoon, around two, telling her he might not be back for supper. "I have a bead on two of the four men," he told her. "Two still unaccounted for."

"What are you planning to do? Confront them?" Worry sat like a block of concrete in the pit of her belly.

"Not yet," he said cryptically. "Gotta go." He hung up before she could ask anything else.

Around four, she finished going through the first set of boxes Lydia had provided and offered to help Lydia with whatever she had planned for dinner. "I'm not a great cook, but I can cut vegetables or toast bread."

"Duly noted," Lydia said with a smile, "but I thought you wanted to take a look at that coded journal."

"I don't have to get to it right away."

"But you want to. I can see it in your bright brown eyes." Lydia laid her hand on Shannon's arm, squeezing gently. "Go ahead. I believe I know how to boil shrimp and bake potatoes without any help."

Shannon took the journal out to the front porch and sat in the wooden rocker, flipping through the pages slowly, looking for any obvious letters. Vowels should have been easy to pick out, but an hour's worth of playing around with the words left Shannon more confused than before.

There might be a second and even third layer of cryptography involved, she knew. Simple codes were too easily broken, so most people who really wanted their information to remain secret applied multiple codes to their documents.

Back home, she had some cryptography books in her collection. Maybe she could call Megan and ask her to stop by her place, grab the books and overnight them to her.

Suppertime came and went without any other word from Gideon. Lydia was trying to pretend she wasn't worried, but Shannon could see the concern in her eyes. As the sun began to drop over the western Gulf of Mexico, Shannon found herself worrying as well.

Why hadn't Gideon called?

TEN MINUTES AFTER he saw four men leave *Ahab's Folly,* heading toward the boardwalk, Gideon had boarded the yacht to take a quick look around. What he found there, however, kept him occupied longer than he'd intended.

From the outside, the boat looked like an ordinary, high-end Azimut yacht. At first flush, the inside looked typical as well, although the furnishings had a distinctly masculine, utilitarian feel to them.

But once he went past the three staterooms and entered what looked to be the crew's quarters, it was as if he'd stepped into an entirely different boat. The crew's quarters had been stripped of beds, the space filled instead with rows of equipment, maps, charts and even a large stash of weapons in a locked glass-front cabinet at one end.

This was a war room. And all the maps and charts seemed to indicate one prime target: Nightshade Island.

He spent longer inside the boat than he'd planned, searching for any sort of identification for the boat's crew, but the only thing he came across that might be any help were papers that indicated *Ahab's Folly* was registered to an entity called AfterAssets, LLC.

He took as many photos as he dared with his cell phone and, with the creeping sensation of time passing far too quickly, scanned the quarters to make sure he hadn't left anything out of place.

Darting a brief look outside to make sure the boat's occupants hadn't returned, Gideon left the yacht and headed up the pier toward the marina exit.

As he bent his head to check the time, he sensed a rush of movement in the twilight gloom. Something slammed into the back of his neck, sending pain jolting all the way down his spine. Staggering around to confront his attacker, he caught a glimpse of the man's face, narrow-featured and twisted with seething resentment. He felt a shock of recognition.

Then something hit him again from behind and he went down, the world going silent and black.

Chapter Seven

"Gideon?"

Gideon opened his eyes, squinting at the beam of light that drove straight into his brain like a knife. He didn't know where he was or why his head was pounding with agony.

The light moved out of his eyes and he saw he was on a pier, surrounded by yachts in their slips and a handful of bystanders watching with curiosity as a Terrebonne Harbor Patrol officer shined a flashlight at him. Hazy memories trickled back. He was at Bay Pointe Marina, looking for the intruders. And he'd found them. Or, to be precise, they'd found him.

In the empty slip nearby, the Azimut was gone. He turned to look out in the harbor, but there were several yachts motoring their way into the bay. *Ahab's Folly* could be almost any of them.

"Are you okay?" The man's voice registered this time. Simon Haley. Gideon and the Harbor Patrol officer had gone fishing together a few times before the general's death had led Gideon to stick closer to Nightshade Island.

Pressing his hand against the back of his head, where the worst of the pain seemed to have settled, Gideon slowly sat up. He felt pretty clearheaded, he decided, and the pain didn't get any worse when he pushed to his feet. "I'm okay, I think," he told Simon.

"What happened?"

He remembered climbing off the boat and coming face-to-face with—

Someone familiar, he thought. He couldn't bring the face to mind, but he had a strong sense that he'd recognized the first man who'd accosted him outside the yacht. He'd never seen the person who'd delivered the knockout blow. "I don't remember much—just a knock on the head." No need to tell Simon about sneaking on the Azimut. Fishing buddy or not, Simon couldn't just turn a blind eye to trespassing.

"How long do you think you've been out?" The question came from someone new—a paramedic, Gideon saw with some dismay. The paramedic came at him with a penlight and once again, needles of light drove into his skull, although not as painful this time.

Gideon looked at his watch. Almost eight-thirty. "No more than five minutes." He'd checked his watch as he was leaving the yacht because he knew Mrs. Ross and Shannon had to be getting worried.

"Pupils look good. Let me look at your head."

"I'm fine," Gideon protested, ducking away from the paramedic's probing hands. *Ahab's Folly* had a head start, and now they knew Gideon was definitely not on Nightshade Island. "I got mugged. I saw nothing. No harm done."

"You could have a concussion," the paramedic protested.

"I've had a concussion before. Believe me, this isn't one." Gideon started walking toward the marina exit, the sense of time slipping away weighing heavily on him, harder to bear than the persistent ache in his head. There were new pains, too, that he was just starting to feel. A hard ache in his rib-cage, and another in the soft tissue of his lower back. Apparently whoever had knocked him out had gotten in a few hard kicks before they left in the Azimut. But none of his injuries was life-threatening.

The same couldn't be said of the yacht moving out in the Gulf, no doubt heading for Nightshade Island.

Simon caught up with Gideon before he'd reached the central pier. "What's going on, man? Is this connected to what happened last night?"

"Probably." He didn't stop walking, forcing Simon to move faster to keep up. "You in a boat or on foot?"

"In a car, actually," Simon said. "You need a lift?"

"Get me to the *Lorelei*. And call in a warning to Harbor Patrol—look for an Azimut motor yacht named *Ahab's Folly*. Don't let it get anywhere near Nightshade Island."

THE CALL FROM Gideon came around nine. He was on the *Lorelei,* on his way back. No need to wait up.

Lydia seemed greatly relieved to hear from him, despite her attempts all evening to pretend she wasn't worried. "He knows I like to get to bed early," she told Shannon, "so he'll probably go straight to the caretaker's house." She paused at the bottom of the stairs to the top floor. "We can relax now, yes?"

Shannon smiled at her. "Yes." Though she wasn't sure she'd really relax until she heard the *Lorelei*'s engine puttering into the boathouse. Too many things could go wrong out on the open water. She'd learned that lesson her very first day on Nightshade Island.

She'd showered earlier and already dressed for bed, mostly as a way to pass the time while she worried about why they hadn't yet heard from Gideon. There was no reason not to tuck herself under the covers of the soft bed and read one of the books she'd loaded onto her e-reader before the trip. Or pull out the coded diary again and give it another shot.

But the sound of a boat engine, distant but growing closer, drew her to the balcony outside her room instead. From where she stood at the railing, she saw the lights of the Hatteras moving slowly toward the boathouse. Relief fluttering in her chest, she watched the boat slide into its slip, disappearing from sight. A few minutes later, Gideon Stone's tall, broad-shouldered figure appeared on the walkway, heading toward Stafford House.

He was moving slowly, she noticed. Limping a little. He stepped into a shaft of moonlight and she could see he was holding his arm against his body, as if favoring his ribs.

He moved out of sight, and she found herself following, moving down the balcony where it wrapped around the house. She turned the corner and caught sight of him again, moving even more slowly now, definitely favoring one side of his body as he limped up the uneven path from the garden to the caretaker's house.

At the door to his house, he paused, pressing his forehead against the door. Alarm clanged in her head as he opened the door and staggered inside.

She stripped off her robe, trading her silk boxer shorts for a pair of jeans. She threw a T-shirt on over her sleeping tank and shoved her feet in a pair of tennis shoes.

Trying to be quiet, she made her way downstairs, not wanting to wake Lydia if she'd already fallen asleep. Slipping out the French doors at the back of the house, she hurried through the garden and up the crooked path to Gideon's house.

GIDEON FELT LIKE hell. Everything hurt, which made him wonder just how many times they'd kicked him around while he was out before they and their co-conspirators made their escape on the Azimut.

At least his vision was clear and his memory seemed mostly intact. There was a minute right after the first blow that was fuzzy. He had a strong sense of having seen someone he recognized, but when he tried to call the man's face to mind, it was a featureless blur.

A sharp rap on the door made him sit up straight, hissing with pain as his sore ribs protested. It could be only Lydia Ross or Shannon Cooper, and he wasn't ready to see either of them tonight.

A second knock came, harder and more insistent than before. Growling with frustration, he pushed to his feet and limped over to the door, swinging it open with more violence than he'd intended.

Shannon took a faltering step back, gazing up at him with wide, worried eyes. A flood of remorse poured through him at her reaction, making him feel like a brute.

He carefully softened his voice. "I thought you'd gone to bed," he said.

Her eyes snapped at him, showing not a whit of her earlier alarm. "Don't know how you'd know, because you didn't even drop by to check on us."

Not in any condition to deal with her at the moment, he stopped trying to appear unthreatening and filled the doorway with his body, blocking her entry. Nor did he tell her he'd spent most of the trip back to Nightshade Island on the horn with fishermen in the area, reassuring himself that a blue-and-white Azimut had come nowhere near the island. "Do you need something?"

She looked him over, as if trying to see past his unwelcoming facade. "What happened in Terrebonne? Did you find out more about the yacht?"

Part of him wanted to shut the door in her face and go lick his wounds in private, but she'd done nothing to deserve that kind of treatment. He backed away, letting her inside. "It's a floating war room," he said, waving at the sofa for her to sit. He took the armchair across from her, trying not to wince in pain.

"Floating war room?" she asked when he didn't immediately continue. "How do you know?"

He gave her a pointed look.

Her eyes widened. "You went aboard?"

"The main part of the yacht is pretty normal. Your typical pleasure boat. Nice decor—a little plain, more for men than women, but nothing to spark any suspicion. But be-lowdecks—"

He described the crew's quarters situation room he'd found. "They had charts of Nightshade Island and the wa-ters around it."

"What are they looking for? Did you get any clue about that?"

He shook his head, then went stock-still, regretting the movement. "If that information was there, it wasn't in plain sight." Grimacing, he pulled his cell phone from his pocket and put it on the low coffee table that sat between them. "I took some pictures. Maybe there's something in there."

Shannon didn't reach for the phone. "You're hurt."

He didn't look at her. The soft sympathy in her voice touched an aching place in the center of his chest, making him feel weak and vulnerable. "I'm fine."

"Rib cage, head—anywhere else?"

He sighed. So much for trying to hide his injuries. Leave it to the nosy little girl detective to see right through him. "There's a place just below my kidneys that feels like it was stomped by a horse," he admitted.

"Someone caught you in the yacht?"

"Just outside," he answered. "It's kind of a blur. I was checking my watch when something hit me on the back of my neck. I turned around and then got coldcocked from behind."

She looked at him with alarm. "You were knocked out?"

"Just for a few minutes."

"You could have a concussion!" She circled the coffee table and crouched in front of him, reaching up to check his eyes.

"I don't have a concussion." He caught her hand, holding it firmly in his large fist. Her skin was soft, her bones deli-cate beneath his fingers. For all her bravado, she could so easily break.

Her brown eyes lifted slowly to meet his, questions shin-ing there, unspoken. The desire to protect her nearly overwhelmed him. But from what? The sharks circling the island, hidden from view?

Or himself?

He quickly let go of her hand, a shiver of panic running through him. "I'm okay, really."

"Let me at least take a look at the damage," she said.

He gazed at her through narrowed eyes, wondering if he dared. "Computer nerd *and* a nurse?"

She smiled. "High-level first aid training is also part of the Cooper Security employee core curriculum."

He gave in. Hell, it was what he wanted anyway, wasn't it? "Most of the damage seems to be upper body. Ribs, soft tissue. I think I have a decent-size bump on the back of my head."

She stood and stepped back, giving him room to strip off his T-shirt. When he looked at her again, she was assessing his body thoroughly. He followed her gaze, taking in his stomach and chest, and saw no sign of bruising.

She looked up at him quickly, a faint pink blush reddening her cheeks. "Nothing obvious on the front side. Let me check your back."

He turned around and heard her suck in a quick breath. "That bad?"

Her footsteps moved closer, until he felt the heat of her body behind him. Her fingertips slid lightly over his back, shooting shivers up his spine. She pressed on a spot a few inches below his shoulder blade and pain galloped across his rib cage, making him gasp.

"Sorry." She ran her hand gently over the ribs beneath the bruise as if to soothe him.

Her touch hurt, but he didn't want her to stop. Even that clinical touch was more than he'd felt from a woman in a long time. Way too long.

"I don't feel an obvious break," she pronounced finally, "but you may have some cracked ribs."

She moved her hand lightly down his back, dipping toward the end of his spine. He sucked in a harsh breath, even though her fingers weren't anywhere near a bruise. His heart thudded loudly in his ears.

"How about here?" she asked, gently probing another bruised area on his lower back.

"It's sore but not terrible." His voice dropped to a growly bass, despite his effort to keep his cool. Her touch was like fire, in a good way.

A very good way.

"You don't remember getting kicked?" she asked.

He shook his head. "I guess they did it after I was down."

"Cowards," she spat through clenched teeth, as if outraged by the thought. He couldn't stop a smile of appreciation from curving his lips, despite his earlier grim mood.

"Am I going to live?" he asked.

He felt her hand move through his hair, her fingers probing the sore spot. She pulled her hand away, leaving him feeling oddly empty. "You're bleeding back here."

He turned to look at her, dropping his gaze to her bloody fingers. Not much there, he saw with relief. "Must not be much more than a scratch."

She crossed into the kitchen and washed the blood off her hands. "Do you have a first aid kit? I can bandage you up."

He trailed after her like a big, stupid, increasingly aroused puppy. "It's in that cabinet."

She turned, her eyes widening at finding him so close. "Wh-which cabinet?"

So he wasn't the only one who felt the delicious tension wrapping its tentacles around them.

Even though he knew he shouldn't, knew he was being provocative, he reached past her to the cabinet next to the sink, his body brushing hers as he leaned forward. He felt a little shudder ripple through her where they touched and bit back a smile of raw male satisfaction.

Her breath was hot and quick against his chest. He closed his eyes, enjoying a brief moment of pleasure, before stepping back, bringing a soft-bodied first aid kit with him. But he didn't move far. As wrong as he knew it was, as dangerous as it felt, he relished seeing the effect his nearness had on Shannon. Drank deeply of the passionate arousal blazing in her dark eyes.

Her lips parted on a shaky breath, but she didn't lower her gaze. He felt himself drowning in her eyes, slipping under her spell with shocking speed. No longer in control, he heard the telltale sound of his doom—the rapid-fire thunder of his pulse in his ears.

He bent his head. She lifted hers.

The first light brush of her mouth to his felt like an electric spark, zinging through his bloodstream. Her mouth parted, her warm breath mingling with his.

He dipped his head again, kissing her more deeply, drinking from the well of passion suddenly overflowing between them. He'd meant to slake his thirst with just a taste, but when her hands clutched his forearms, and her body rose, soft but fierce, to flatten against his, he felt the weakening threads of his control beginning to snap and tear.

He roped his arm around her, driving her back against the edge of the sink. Her breath exploded in his mouth, a gasp of pain, and she tightened her grip on his forearms.

He let her go immediately, stepping back in horror.

She stared back at him, confusion written all over her face.

He turned away with a jerk, shaken by the rapid loss of his tightly held control. "Let's get this done," he growled, angry at himself and, illogically, at her for making him feel the way he did right now, hot and aching for something he didn't dare let himself have. He hurried back to the front room, taking the first aid kit with him.

He sat down again, digging in the kit's inner pockets for bandages. By the time she reached where he sat, she looked composed and cool, taking the bottle of antiseptic and sterile cleansing pads he handed her with steady hands. So calm was she, in fact, that he wondered if he'd merely dreamed the kiss that had ripped his world asunder.

She went behind his chair and examined his head again, her touch light. "Whatever hit you split the skin." She started wiping antiseptic on the wound, making it sting. "It's not deep. You're lucky it didn't bleed even more—head wounds can be real gushers."

"No stitches needed?"

"I don't think so. It's not even bleeding much anymore." She spread some sort of ointment across the scratch and stepped back. "I don't think you even need a bandage. Just be sure to clean it regularly."

He closed the first aid kit and laid it on the table. "Thanks."

"You're welcome." Her eyes narrowed. "What do you plan to do about the yacht you found?"

"I told a friend in the Harbor Patrol. He's got his boats keeping an eye out for it."

"I looked into the RIB you mentioned—the Zodiac Bayrunner? It can't go far without refueling. Engine's just not big enough and it eats a lot of gas." She sat on the sofa again, her hands flexing in her lap. He forced himself not to meet her curious gaze, unable—or maybe just unwilling—to answer the unspoken questions in her dark eyes.

"They may have other avenues of approach besides the Zodiac," he warned. "From what I saw in the crew's quarters, these people aren't messing around. They want to get on this island in a bad way. They want to get inside Stafford House in a bad way."

"I wish Lydia would head to the mainland where she'd be better protected." As soon as the words escaped her mouth, she looked appalled. "I didn't mean—you've done an amazing job of taking care of her—"

"But I can't be here all the time," he said flatly, not offended. He'd tried to convince Lydia to consider an early move himself with as little effect. "Mrs. Ross doesn't really want to leave at all, but the state has made her a generous offer, and she knows she'll be far more independent on the mainland. But that doesn't mean she wants to leave a minute earlier than she has to. Nightshade Island's been her home nearly her whole life."

Shannon looked wistful, her expression tugging at his curiosity. But he refused to ask her what she was thinking about. He wasn't going to let himself get sucked any deeper into her life than their temporary isolation together on the island required.

That horse is out of the barn, cowboy.

He shook off the taunting voice in the back of his mind, the one that sounded entirely too much like his father's. "I appreciate your coming here to help me out. Really. Thanks for the first aid."

"But get lost?" she said.

"It's been a long day. I could use a shower and some shut-eye."

She pushed to her feet, drawing his gaze to her again. He'd found her cute the day before, dressed up in her prim little suit and snapping her angry eyes at him, but this Shannon Cooper, soft and sweet-smelling in faded jeans and worn cotton T-shirt, was pure temptation. More womanly than youthful, softly sexy rather than coltishly adorable.

Even more dangerous.

"We're not going to talk about what just happened, are we?"

He shook his head. "We're going to forget it."

She shot him a wry smile. "I have a good memory." But she didn't protest as he walked her to the door, torturing himself with his rigid self-control. He didn't reach over to tuck behind her ear the loose lock of hair that had escaped her messy ponytail. He didn't catch her hand as she stepped onto the porch or beg her to stay a little longer.

He didn't lean against the door after he shut it behind her, wishing she'd stayed.

Not for long anyway.

He went directly to the shower and ran the water as cool as he dared, even though it would do little to soothe his aches and bruises. Within a couple of minutes, he'd had all he could take. Shivering, he exited the tub and briskly toweled himself dry, not bothering with dressing as he headed into his darkened bedroom.

As he pulled back the covers of his bed, a flicker of movement outside caught his attention. He crossed to the window and quickly realized the flash of white he'd seen was Shannon Cooper's T-shirt, glowing in the cool moonlight as she walked carefully up the darkened trail to the lighthouse.

What the hell was she doing?

She circled the lighthouse, bending at one point to pick up something. A second later, a narrow beam of light cut through the darkness, drawing a small circle of illumination against the time-worn stone of the lighthouse wall.

Her penlight. She'd said she'd dropped it when she was in the lighthouse the night before.

He watched, waiting for her to reverse course and move back down the path toward his house. But as she turned to do just that, she stopped, her head craning to look upward.

He followed her gaze and saw only the darkened windows of the service room and the reflection of moonlight on the glass that enclosed the lantern room. But whatever had drawn her attention upward held it, luring her toward the lighthouse entrance.

She disappeared into the gloom inside.

Chapter Eight

Shannon had seen nothing out of the ordinary. No flicker of movement in the windows, no flash of color, no ghostly hand against the lantern room window. Nor had she heard anything more substantial than the whisper of the Gulf breeze through the dry fingers of sea grass growing hip-high around the base of the lighthouse.

But the hair on the back of her neck rose, a warning sign that something in the lighthouse was different.

If this were a horror movie, she thought as she eased her way toward the lighthouse entrance, there'd be a man with a butcher's knife just inside, poised to make the pretty but dim heroine pay for being too stupid to live.

But this wasn't a horror movie, and she'd seen herself today how seriously the local fishermen and even the Harbor Patrol had taken their roles as gatekeepers. No way had a Zodiac Bayrunner gotten anywhere near Nightshade Island today.

This is really about regaining honor, isn't it, Cooper? Last night you got spooked and ran like a little girl.

Well, so what if it was? The only way something retained the power to frighten a person was if she let it, right? The lighthouse had spooked her last night. Tonight, she would conquer her fear and rob the creepy old place of any power over her.

The penlight painted a pale streak of illumination across

the old stone walls of the spiral staircase and speared the darkness overhead as she directed the beam upward. There was only stillness above, as far as she could see. No floating wraith of the old lightkeeper. No gremlins waiting in the shadows to dash her down the stairs to the stone floor below.

She was pleased with how normally she was breathing when she reached the service room. A little winded from the exertion, her heart rate up a little, but not bad at all. She doubted any of her brothers could have managed the climb in the dark any better.

Without the press of dangerous invaders and a ticking clock to drive her into haste, she took a good look around the service room. It was dusty. Draped with cobwebs. Dank and cool, drafty where the wind moaned through the cracked window and the narrow space beneath the door.

She looked at the closed door. Had she closed it last night? She didn't remember whether she had or not.

She flashed the beam toward the far wall, where a small light about the size of a pinhead glowed red. It was part of a switch connected to a cast-iron box that seemed to disappear into the wall where the foghorns emerged on the other side.

The mechanism was on. Had it been on last night?

Definitely not when she entered the service room. She'd have noticed the light shining in the gloom. And she'd been too freaked out to notice anything but the fastest way out of the room after the horn went off.

At least everything seemed to be working now. Maybe there'd been a short. Or the connector might be loose, which made it susceptible to coming apart again.

She studied the switch mechanisms under the penlight and made sure anything that connected to anything else was firmly seated. Nothing seemed particularly loose.

She stood very still, just taking in the atmosphere. Musty

air filled her nostrils, with just a hint of the salty sea blowing in on the breeze.

And something else.

Gun oil, she realized. Reminiscent of Gideon sitting at the kitchen table at Stafford House, cleaning his Walther.

She closed her eyes, the image of him still imprinted on her brain—Gideon, standing there in the caretaker's house, stripped to the skin and about the most intensely masculine thing she'd ever seen. Dark hair had curled across his sternum, narrowing to a dark line that intersected his belly and dipped beneath the waistband of his jeans. He had a flat, toned abdomen and wide, powerful shoulders, his body well-proportioned without looking overmuscled. His skin was lightly tanned and nicked here and there with the souvenirs of a life in the military, scars large and small, including a Marine Corps insignia tattooed on his left deltoid muscle and a surgical scar in the shadowy valley beneath his left pectoral muscle that suggested a close brush with not making it back alive.

If she'd plugged her ideal parameters for the perfect male body into a computer search engine, she didn't think she could have come up with a better representative sample. She'd tried not to stare, but his sheer, imposing masculinity was a thing of beauty.

And when they'd kissed, oh so briefly—

Enough. She opened her eyes and looked around the empty service room, grounding herself in the stark reality. He'd stopped the kiss. He didn't want things between them to go any further, and that was fine with her. She was there to do a job, not to moon over a big, surly stranger built like a superhero.

She made it to the ground floor without stumbling. And if she felt the hair on the back of her neck prickling, as if unseen eyes followed her all the way to the ground, well, that was just her silly imagination.

BY THE TIME Gideon had pulled on jeans and a T-shirt, Shannon's penlight reappeared up in the service room, outlining her slim silhouette as she moved about inside.

She was still up there when he slipped out his back door and started up the crooked path to the lighthouse, his body protesting in creaks and groans, like a rusty engine forced into use. As he neared the lighthouse, the light disappeared. He heard the sound of her footsteps ringing on the metal stairway as he neared the entrance and had to step back as she emerged from inside, her stride forceful, as if she were on a mission.

She skidded to a sudden stop as he loomed up in the dark, slumping back against the lighthouse wall. "You scared the hell out of me!"

"Sorry." He sort of meant it. Mostly. Even though he still wanted to know what she was doing climbing to the top of the lighthouse in the middle of the night.

"I thought you were going to bed."

"I thought you were, too," he replied, ruthlessly ignoring the mental image that arose from thinking about Shannon Cooper and a bed in the same sentence. "What were you doing up there?"

She flashed a sheepish smile that made his stomach turn flips. "Exorcising ghosts."

"Ghosts?"

"I got freaked out last night while I was up there and the horn sounded. Ran away like a big baby." Her chin lifted. "I felt the need to prove to myself that I could go back there and be okay."

"And did you?"

She nodded. "While I was up there, I checked the connectors on the foghorn. Everything looks as if it's pretty tightly seated. All the connections were solid. I'm not sure why it didn't sound last night."

He felt a ripple of shame at not thinking to check the connectors himself that morning before he left the island. What if the switch hadn't worked again, leaving Shannon and Lydia without any way to call for help?

"You look dead on your feet." Shannon closed her hand around his elbow, nudging him toward the path. "You should be in bed."

His body concurred with her, though probably not in the spirit she'd intended. "I'll walk you back to Stafford House."

"It's not necessary."

He was beginning to think it was. If only to exorcise his own ghosts.

Shannon Cooper had become a powerful temptation to him, a distraction from his mission to protect Lydia Ross and her husband's legacy. He'd almost let a kiss derail him from that mission entirely. He needed to prove to himself he could handle having her around without letting his libido get the best of him.

"Maybe you should reconsider staying there," Shannon said as they neared Gideon's house. "Safety in numbers."

"You afraid to be there alone?"

She turned to look at him, her eyes shining in the moonlight. "Actually, I'd like to have you where I can check on you. That's a pretty big lump on the back of your head."

"I'm—"

"Fine," she finished for him with a frustrated sigh. "Maybe you are. But if you're not, I'd like you to be where you can call for help and someone might actually hear you."

He knew she was right. While he was fairly sure he didn't have a concussion—he'd experienced no double vision and very little head pain—it would be obstinate and stupid not to take precautions. A closed head injury was nothing to mess around with.

"Okay," he said. "Let me grab some clothes."

She walked with him up to the porch but dropped onto

the double bench that sat outside his door. "I'll wait here and enjoy the view." She waved out toward the moonlit water.

He followed her gaze, taking in the glittering Gulf of Mexico, bathed silvery blue by moonlight. It was beautiful. Mysterious. Full of hidden depths. His gaze slid back to Shannon Cooper's face, realizing the same could be said of the serene, composed young woman sitting on his porch. Even though his whole body seemed to vibrate whenever he was near her—all the worse now after their brief kiss—she showed little sign of being affected by his nearness at all.

Was it an act? Or was she truly unaffected by their fleeting moment of intimacy?

Suddenly annoyed, he pushed through the front door and shoved a change of clothes into a canvas duffel. He put the first aid kit inside as well and returned to the porch. Shannon still sat on the bench, her head resting against the wall. Her eyes were closed and her breathing was slow and even.

He hated to wake her, but he could hardly leave her out here to nap all night. "Shannon?"

Her eyes snapped open, unfocused. She finally spotted him and shot him a sheepish grin that made his heart flip. "Sorry. Long day."

"Tell me about it," he murmured, holding out his hand to help her up.

She stared at his outstretched hand for a moment, indecision evident in her expression. But she lifted her hand, finally, placing it in his. Her gaze rose to meet his, vulnerability shining in her dark eyes.

So she had been affected, he thought, unable to fully quell a feeling of sheer masculine pleasure.

He closed his fingers around hers, careful to be gentle, and tugged lightly, pulling her to her feet. It took all his strength not to pull her closer and finish what they'd started in his kitchen earlier.

He loosened his grip on her hand, and she let her fingers slide away from his. An ache settled low in his belly as she moved forward, down the stairs, putting distance between them.

Slowly, he followed her down the garden path to Stafford House.

"You should have come straight here last night!" Lydia's voice was firm but affectionate as she took the plate Gideon handed her. "You could have had a concussion."

Shannon glanced at Gideon, surprised he'd even told his employer about what happened to him on the dock at Bay Pointe Marina. Gideon's gaze slid across hers, settling for a second, before turning back to Lydia, who sat next to him at the table and unfolded a napkin across her lap.

"I'm fine," he said. Shannon stifled a laugh.

"Well, at least Shannon had the good sense to talk you into staying here last night. I shudder to think what might have happened had you passed out at the caretaker's house. All alone with nobody to help you—" She paused in the middle of slicing her waffle, angling her head to take another look at the egg-size lump on the back of his head. "Does it hurt terribly?"

"Only when you touch it," he said lightly. "So don't touch it."

Lydia chuckled. "Duly noted."

They ate their waffles in silence for a few minutes, enjoying a quiet camaraderie that Shannon found soothing. Her experience with family breakfasts leaned more toward the loud and boisterous.

Gideon took their empty plates to the sink, waving off their offers to handle the cleanup. He rinsed the plates with dish soap and water and placed them in the drying rack.

"How did you sleep?" Shannon asked when he returned to the table.

"Like the dead." He dropped into his chair.

"Don't say that." Lydia looked appalled.

He looked mortified. "I'm sorry."

She laid a forgiving hand on his shoulder. "No, I'm being a superstitious old woman." She dropped her hand away and stood. "I believe I'm going out to the garden this morning. I've neglected my poor babies in all this excitement." She looked at Shannon. "Have you showed Gideon the coded diary yet?"

Gideon looked at Shannon. "Coded diary?"

Shannon had brought the book down with her that morning, spending a little time on the front porch enjoying the morning air and trying to make some headway with the cipher. She went to the coffee table to retrieve the journal, showing it to Gideon as Lydia headed out to the garden.

"Lydia said it's definitely the general's handwriting," she told him as he thumbed through the pages. "Does the code look at all familiar to you?"

He gave her a wry look. "If it looks familiar, it's not good code."

She smiled. "I have some books at home on cryptography—" At his perplexed expression, she added, "It's a hobby."

His dimples came out to play. "I suppose you also do open heart surgery and build cold fusion reactors in your spare time?"

"I'm a computer geek, remember? Code is my life."

"Not quite the same sort of code." He frowned as he looked down at one of the pages.

"Did you find something?"

"I'm not sure," he admitted. "It's just—this word looks familiar."

She went around the table and looked over his shoulder. His index finger was pointing to a series of five letters. *VETCA*.

"Vetca?" she said aloud.

"I've heard that term used before. I'm just not sure where."

"Could it be a foreign word?"

He shook his head. "No, I don't think so. This book is definitely in code, not a foreign language."

His brow furrowed as if he were in pain. She reached across the table and put her hand on his arm, trying not to notice the crisp hair tickling her fingers or the way his sinewy muscles flexed at her touch. "Are you sure you're fine?"

He looked up at her. "My ribs hurt like hell."

She smiled. "Must be really bad for you to admit it."

"Probably should have taped them up last night." He handed the book back to her. "I'm not sure what this is about. I'll give some thought to where I've seen the word *vetca* before." He stood from the table, moving a little gingerly. "Yeah, definitely should have taped them."

She rose with him. "I can do it for you."

He slanted her a wry look. "I don't think that's a good idea."

The air between them heated immediately, supercharged by his frank admission. "Because of what happened last night?"

"I'm not looking for that kind of entanglement."

"Neither am I," she said quickly, wishing she sounded a little less tentative. "It's hard enough trying to convince my brother I can handle a field assignment without complicating it with—" She faltered, searching for the right word.

"A complication," he supplied wryly.

"A complication," she agreed.

He just nodded, as if they'd said all that needed saying. "Lydia doesn't remember, because of all the chaos, I guess, but she has a hair appointment in Terrebonne later this morning."

"You remember her hair appointments?" she asked with surprise. Talk about taking a caretaker's job seriously.

"It's written on the calendar next to the fridge," he said with a dimpled grin that almost made her forget their recent agreement to ignore their attraction. "Do you want to stay

here and go through more boxes or come with us?" His tone
was almost wheedling, as if he was consciously tempting her
to play hooky from work and come play.

And she *had* gotten through more of the general's papers
yesterday than she'd thought she could accomplish in that
short time....

"Why not?" she asked with a grin. "Let's go to Terrebonne."

Chapter Nine

"Have you ever been here before?" Lydia asked Shannon as they walked the short distance from Terrebonne Marina to the marina's rental garage where she and Gideon kept their vehicles.

"Just through town to get to the marina," she admitted. "But my cousin spent some time here a while ago. His first wife grew up here, and his new wife, Natalie, used to work here as a sheriff's deputy."

Lydia gave her a quick, interested look. "Natalie Becker?"

"Yes. Natalie Cooper now—she and J.D. married up in Gossamer Ridge a few months ago."

"Becker Oil Becker?" Gideon asked with a low whistle.

"I believe so," Shannon said. Her cousin-in-law came from family money, she knew, though neither J.D. nor Natalie talked about it.

Gideon unlocked the padlock on the garage unit and pulled open the large, wide doors, letting daylight illuminate the dark interior. Side by side in the well-maintained garage, a cream-colored Cadillac and a big black Ford F-150 made an odd pair. No question who drove what, either, although it was Gideon who unlocked the Caddy and slid behind the wheel, apparently willing to play chauffeur to Lydia as well as take care of Nightshade Island.

Shannon sat in the back, behind Lydia, and watched with

interest as they pulled onto Terrebonne's tiny, oak-lined main drag and drove into the center of the small coastal town.

Redbrick city buildings filled one side of the central square, across the street from a small green park, where oaks, hickories and magnolias dripped with Spanish moss, setting a picture-postcard scene of somnolent Southern charm. Gideon parked the Caddy in front of a small store a block down Main Street, with a plate glass storefront sign, crimson letters outlined in white, proclaiming Pamela's Style Salon lay inside.

"Pam and the other ladies will take good care of me," Lydia said firmly when both Shannon and Gideon showed signs of sticking around the salon to wait for her. "Go show Shannon around town."

Shannon thought about arguing because the last thing she wanted to do was spend the day trying to pretend she didn't find Gideon Stone maddeningly attractive. But she also had a fascination for small towns, taking any chance she got to explore them.

"Okay, but you stay right here."

Gideon added. "Don't budge from here until we come back."

Lydia's exasperation shone from her bright eyes, but she agreed to stay put. "No need to hurry—I have a lot of catching up to do!"

Shannon followed Gideon outside. They left the Caddy locked in front of the hair salon and walked up Main Street.

"Terrebonne was originally a French settlement, stragglers who left Fort Louis before the flood and struck off on their own," Gideon told her, his tone almost formal, as if he took his role as tour guide seriously. "In the early eighteenth century, most of the settlers fell in a battle with the Choctaw Indians, who took over Terrebonne for a while. Then, after the French abandoned flood-prone Fort Louis and built Fort Conde, more Frenchmen came through, this time armed and ready, and drove the Choctaws out."

Shannon looked around the pretty town. "What was the appeal?"

"Good fishing on Terrebonne Bay. Good hunting in the woods north of town." He quirked a smile at her. "Great place for smugglers to land by sea, unnoticed by the bigger settlement in Fort Conde."

"Ah," she said with an answering smile. "Filthy lucre."

"Not so filthy when it stands between you and starvation, I suppose."

They walked a half mile or so down the main street, coming eventually to a small bookstore tucked in the middle of nowhere down a side street. "They probably won't have cryptography books here," he warned as he led her under the green awning over the front door, "but it won't hurt to look."

Inside, the bookstore had the delightfully cluttered air of a real bibliophile's lair. Old books, new books, tiny old rare books tucked into locked glass cabinets and large picture books for children lying open on tables, inviting little book lovers to browse.

They looked around without luck for a book on cryptography, although the helpful clerk offered to order one for her. Shannon declined, but she made the clerk smile by picking up a couple of thrillers she'd been meaning to buy for weeks. They left the shop behind, dropped off the books at the Caddy and headed back to the hair salon to check on Lydia.

Lydia was still waiting for her turn in one of the salon chairs, but she was clearly enjoying the chatty atmosphere of the salon, in no hurry to leave. "Take the Caddy and drive down the bay road," she suggested to Gideon, who shook his head with a long-suffering smile and did as she asked.

Shannon buckled herself into the front seat next to him, checking her phone for messages. She'd turned it off that morning because the office was apparently experiencing some IT trouble, and all the agents felt the need to copy her on any texts or emails they sent to her assistant. The constant beeps had been driving her crazy.

She thumbed through the older messages, deleting most. When she reached the most recent, a text from her brother Rick, the stark message caught her by surprise. "Call me," it said. "Important."

She hit her brother's number on the speed dial. He answered on the second ring. "Shannon, where have you been? I messaged you an hour ago." Rick's gravelly voice was more impatient than panicked, making her relax a little bit. At least there didn't seem to be a family emergency.

"I was getting a boatload of texts about an IT problem I can't deal with from here. Tell everyone to stop copying me!"

"Okay, will do. Listen, Jesse told me about that boat Gideon Stone found at the Bay Pointe Marina."

"Right, *Ahab's Folly.*" Gideon looked up at her words. The intensity of his gaze was unnerving. "Did you find out anything about it?" she asked Rick.

"The registration number you sent is phony. It's a Texas registration number, but not one in their system."

"Who're you talking to?" Gideon asked, sounding suspicious.

She covered the receiver. "My brother Rick. I sent the information about the Azimut to my brother Jesse to look into."

"You might have asked me."

"You were asleep." She removed her hand. "I can't say I'm surprised it's a fake number," she told her brother.

"We also looked into AfterAssets," Rick went on. "And this is where it gets kind of scary. AfterAssets, LLC, is registered to a firm in Farmville, Virginia. A firm that, as far as we can tell, consists of a single-room building in the middle of nowhere that doesn't even seem to have electricity or a phone physically on the premises."

"A dummy company."

"Yeah, looks like it. But we did a little more digging, and guess who signed the LLC registration?"

"Who?"

"Our old friend Salvatore Beckett."

"SALVATORE BECKETT?" THE hair on the back of Gideon's neck crawled as Shannon ended her short summary of her brother's call.

"He was part of a secret, illegal section at a security company called MacLear Security," Shannon began.

"I know about the Special Services Unit," he interrupted. "Beckett's involved with AfterAssets, LLC? Isn't he in jail?"

"He wasn't at the time of the company's registration in Virginia," Shannon answered, looking queasy. "If this company really is connected to the SSU—"

"Was AfterAssets an offshoot of MacLear?" His gut was beginning to ache, tight with anxiety. If the SSU was behind what happened on Nightshade Island two nights ago, it explained a lot, including the yacht, the military-style RIB and the black-clad commandos.

He was surprised they hadn't just shot their way in. Was there a reason they'd been circumspect?

"I don't think so," she answered. "It registered for business in January of last year, about two months after MacLear disbanded."

"AfterAssets," he said aloud. "Assets after—"

"After MacLear went belly-up."

"They probably hid the assets of their dirty jobs," Gideon said with a grim nod. "And now they're laundering that money and whatever new money they're earning through AfterAssets."

"At least we know Barton Reid isn't getting his hands on any of that money." Shannon grimaced. "The courts froze his assets pending his trial, except for his legal fund."

Barton Reid. The man's name was like poison in Gideon's

ears. The former State Department official had been impli-
cated in a conspiracy to commit dozens of murders and attempted murders, many of which had dangerously escalated
existing tensions in war-torn countries where American forces
were involved in missions.

He was a traitor as far as Gideon was concerned. Life in
prison was too good for him.

He stared out at the Gulf of Mexico, where the first stirring
of whitecaps warned of the tropical storm roiling inexorably
closer to the mainland. They had two days, maybe three, before the storm started making trouble. Evacuation from the
island might even be necessary if the storm was powerful
enough to threaten a storm surge.

He didn't know if it was safer to be on the island or stuck
in a mainland motel riding it out, considering they had no
idea who was behind the attacks on Nightshade Island. Or
what, specifically, they were looking for.

The general hadn't lived to tell him that part of the tale.

"You know something about this," Shannon said, eerily
perceptive.

"About what?" he hedged.

"You don't seem surprised to hear that the SSU could be
behind this mess. Why is that?"

He didn't look at her. "They're a nasty bunch."

"So's the South Boston mob, but I'd be pretty damned surprised to hear they were sending goons to infiltrate Nightshade Island," she said flatly. "What do you know about the
SSU? What do they want?"

"I don't know," he said truthfully.

"But you have some ideas."

He sighed. "Some," he admitted.

She didn't say anything for an uncomfortably long moment. He sneaked a look at her and found her gazing out the
windshield, her expression thoughtful. "Lydia said her son
died saving your life."

Pain, edged with bitter regret, ripped another hole in his soul. "He did."

"She didn't say so, but you must have come here not long afterward. Probably injured, right?"

He didn't answer, but he didn't deny it.

"Injured badly enough that you couldn't go right back to the battlefield." She looked at him, her gaze dropping to his chest. "You have a scar under your chest. A surgical scar, scary close to your heart."

He looked down, remembering those bleak days two years ago, after Ford Ross's death, when he'd feared his friend's sacrifice would have been for nothing at all. He'd been in intensive care at Landstuhl Regional Medical Center on the Ramstein Air Base, too unstable to be shipped home to Bethesda yet. That he'd made it out of Kaziristan to Ramstein at all had been a bloody miracle.

"I lost crazy amounts of blood," he said aloud, remembering the unreality of what his doctor had told him once he'd been on the mend. "Five times my body's volume. They just kept pumping blood back inside me until they could repair the nick in my aorta."

He heard her murmur of dismay.

"Shrapnel from the grenade," he added. "A fluke, really." Ford's body armor had taken the brunt of the blast, but not all of it. "I already had a leg wound, so when the grenade landed on top of us, I couldn't crawl away fast enough."

"And Ford threw himself on the grenade." She sounded sick.

"There was no time to think. He just acted."

He felt her soft fingers on his arm. He looked over at her and saw she was teary-eyed. "I'm sorry. For Ford and for you. What you do, the risks you take to protect this country—"

"What we did," he corrected gently. "By the time I was well enough to return to duty if I pushed it, General Ross had given me an assignment I couldn't refuse."

"An assignment?"

"I guess I should start at the beginning," he said quietly, wondering if he was crazy to share what he was about to say with a woman who was a virtual stranger. "See, when I went into the marines, it was because I had literally nowhere else to go." An image of his father's blood-spattered face and hands filled Gideon's mind, as horrific now as it had been the day he walked in on the scene. He heard his father's words, flat and unemotional. *One day you'll understand, son. You'll see how she drove me to it, just to shut her up. You're just like me, you know.*

He shuddered, deep inside, but fought not to let Shannon see it. "I told you my father killed my mom—"

"So you weren't just saying that to shut me up?"

Her words made him flinch, but he managed to look at her. "No."

Her fingers tightened on his arm. "I'm so sorry. What happened to your father?"

"He was sent up—life without parole in a South Carolina state prison. I guess he's still there. I haven't seen him since I was sixteen." He tried to keep his voice even. "I suppose someone would have called to let me know if he'd died."

"I can't even imagine—" She blinked, and the tears welling on her lower lids spilled down her cheeks. "What happened to you? Did you have someone to take you in? Did you have any brothers and sisters?"

"Just me," he said flatly. "I'm glad of that. I wouldn't wish the experience of being Buck Stone's offspring on anyone else."

There were mornings, when he looked in the mirror bleary-eyed and unshaven, that Gideon saw his father's face staring back at him. The same square jaw and cold blue eyes. The same barely leashed violence lurking behind the deceptively placid features.

"Did you go to foster care?" The squeeze of Shannon's hand on his arm drew him back from a dark internal place.

"Stayed with my uncle until his fishing business went belly up and he couldn't afford a second mouth to feed. Then I joined the marines." And channeled his aggression in war against hardened, vicious enemies instead of innocent women and children.

But now that he was a civilian again—

"And then you were shot."

He nodded. "After I was stable enough to leave Landstuhl for the States, there was nobody waiting for me. Except General Ross." One of his first memories, upon waking up in the hospital in Bethesda, was the general's kind, time-worn face. Doctors told him later that the general had arrived before Gideon himself, informed through the military grapevine of the overseas transport bringing Gideon stateside. He'd made a point to be there, to greet the marine whose life his son's heroic death had spared. "General Ross asked me to join him and his wife on Nightshade Island to recuperate. I thought then he might have wanted a substitute son, at least for a little while, to help ease the constant pain of losing Ford."

"That's clearly how Lydia sees you."

He managed a smile. "I'll never be Ford."

"I don't think that's what she wants from you." Shannon's voice was gentle. A little careful. "She would really like it if you called her Lydia instead of Mrs. Ross, you know."

"I can't," he said, regret shredding his insides.

"Why?"

He didn't want to talk about what he felt. What he didn't want to let himself feel. He didn't want to talk at all, but he'd started this story.

He had to finish it.

"General Ross thought there was someone high in the government involved in manipulating world events to suit some unnamed purpose," he said flatly. "Someone even higher than Barton Reid."

Shannon remained quiet. Too quiet. He dared a quick glance at her and saw her gazing through the windshield, her expression entirely unreadable. Her stillness unnerved him.

"None of this is coming as any surprise to you."

"Her name was kept out of the papers," she said after a moment. "But earlier this year, Barton Reid sent SSU assassins to kill my sister-in-law Amanda, who used to work for the CIA. And another group of the SSU went after my sister Megan when she was trying to prove ties between Reid and her husband's death."

"Vince Randall," he murmured, feeling sick. "I heard about that. But I didn't know his wife was a Cooper."

"You think the island intruders were SSU agents, don't you?"

"I think they're connected with them, yes," he admitted. "They're riding around in a boat owned by a company connected to Salvatore Beckett, who was a squad leader in the SSU. Their tactics and equipment are similar to what we know of the SSU."

"So what would the SSU want from Lydia?"

"The only thing I can think of is the general's papers. Or maybe even that journal you found."

"Is there some damning evidence against the SSU in there?"

"I didn't think so." The general had let him in on a lot of his suspicions, but he'd always sensed the old soldier was keeping some things to himself. Maybe his theories were too volatile to see the light of day without a lot more proof behind them. General Ross had certainly shared his information with Gideon on a need-to-know basis.

"The general brought you to Nightshade Island for more than just recuperation, didn't he?"

Her quick mind seemed to leap past the carefully vague

things he told her to get right to the heart of the situation. "As it turns out, yes."

"What did he want?"

"He wanted me to help him prove that the SSU launched the grenade that killed Ford."

Chapter Ten

"Lydia doesn't know the general had questions about Ford's death." Gideon slid his hand under Shannon's elbow as they walked.

She tried to ignore the fire his touch ignited and concentrated on his words. "I'm not sure it's fair to keep that kind of information from her. You're talking about her son."

"She's lost so much already. What if the general was wrong?"

"Do you think he was wrong?" Shannon looked up at him.

He stopped walking, turning to face her fully. "I don't know."

"Lydia has a right to know that her husband thought her son was murdered. You should tell her what you do know."

He looked miserable. "I'll think about it."

She laid her hand on his chest. "Don't wait too long."

He covered her hand with his palm. "I'll think about it," he repeated. He drew her hand away from his chest but didn't let go. Hand in hand, they walked up the street toward the hair salon.

"Why did the general think the SSU was behind Ford's death?"

"For three weeks before his death, Ford had been working a special assignment for the head of the Marine Corps forces in Kaziristan. General Ross couldn't give me any details about the assignment, but he did tell me that intel agents for all four service branches had begun to suspect that there were rogue elements within MacLear. They were trying to put together a case to end all Defense Department contracts with the company."

"That would have bankrupted MacLear, wouldn't it?" Shannon knew MacLear's primary source of income had been its lucrative contracts with the U.S. Department of Defense.

"Yes."

Shannon's breath caught in her throat. "Oh, my God."

Gideon turned to look at her. "What?"

"Vince," she murmured. "My sister's late-husband. What if the SSU thought his investigations were sanctioned by army intel? Could that be what got him killed?"

"I don't think any of the armed services were investigating MacLear that far back. Although—" Gideon frowned. "General Ross told me the questions about MacLear first arose about four years ago. "

"So maybe Vince's death got the ball rolling?"

"Maybe so." Gideon sighed. "If we could break the code in the general's journal, we'd probably know a lot more."

"I need to tell Jesse about your theory," Shannon said quietly a few minutes later.

"No."

"You don't trust my brother?"

"I don't *know* your brother."

"But you know me."

"No, I don't." He stopped walking and ran his free hand through his hair, frustration crinkling his face. "I met you two days ago. It's crazy that I've told you as much as I already have."

She looked down at their joined hands. He must have followed her gaze, for he released her hand and crossed his arms over his chest.

"I have a stake in this." She kept her voice quiet but firm. "Maybe even bigger than yours."

His lips flattened to a line. "You'd be safer back home."

A flare of anger burned up the back of her neck. "Excuse me?"

"I think you should go back home and let me handle things from here."

She shook her head. "Like hell. Lydia hired me. She's the only one who can fire me."

Uncrossing his arms, he caught her shoulders in his big, strong hands and drew her closer. "If those guys who came onto the island the other night really are SSU agents, they're not playing around. They may be trying to avoid open conflict at the moment, but if they're pushed, they'll kill. You should know that by now."

She tried to ignore the shivery flood of attraction turning her limbs to jelly. It wasn't merely physical, though she couldn't deny the slightest touch from him could set her blood on fire. Gideon Stone was the real deal—hero material. Strong, smart, driven and fiercely loyal to the people who'd been kind and loyal to him. Shannon had grown up among such men, knew the value of them. The rarity.

"I know a lot about the SSU," she said aloud, fighting for focus. "I've made it a point to learn everything I can about them so I'll be prepared if I ever come face-to-face with one of them."

"You can't prepare enough."

"I'm prepared enough to back you up," she insisted, flattening her hands against his chest, intending to push away from his distracting grasp. But at his swift intake of breath at her touch, she lost her train of thought.

His eyes dilated until there was only a narrow rim of blue around the pupils. "Lydia's not the only one who's lost everything, Shannon. My job on the battlefield was to protect my fellow marines. That's what we think about out there, you know? Home, family, country—those are abstracts. You fight and you die for the guy in the foxhole with you. That's your goal. And I failed. I was already hurt. I should have been the one who covered the grenade. Ford should have been the one to live."

She shook her head, horrified. "Don't say that."

"I came here to Alabama to help the general. I was supposed to protect him and Mrs. Ross, but I failed to do that, too. Now he's gone and I have no idea if I'm going to be able to keep the wolves away from Lydia, either."

"You just called her Lydia."

He blinked, as if confused by her words.

"You don't want to get close to her. You think if you get close to someone, you put them in danger. So you put up walls—"

"Stop." He gave her a light shake, then jerked his hands away from her shoulders, looking appalled. "I'm sorry."

She was shaking, she realized with some surprise. Trembling like a leaf. The sheer intensity of emotions roiling through her overwhelmed her—frustration, anger, pity, fear, and underlying it all, an unexpected, overpowering affection for this complicated, impossible man.

"Why are you sorry?" she asked carefully, although she already suspected she knew the answer. It was written all over his tormented, guilty face.

"I shouldn't have put my hands on you."

"You didn't hurt me."

He looked away. "I could have."

Carefully, she touched him. He shook her hand away. "Let's go find Lydia."

They walked the rest of the way to the hair salon in silence, keeping a safe, careful distance from each other. Shannon hoped Lydia would be ready to go back to the island, where Shannon could distract herself with work.

But Lydia was in the middle of a manicure when they arrived, with a pedicure to follow. She smiled apologetically to them as they entered the small salon. "I'm afraid I couldn't say no—Lori just got a new color in." She waved her hands at Shannon, showing off a pearly pink polish. "The girls are going out for sandwiches from the deli down the street. I'll get something with them."

"We've been telling Lydia all the town gossip," the manicurist, a blonde in her early thirties, told Shannon with a friendly smile. "We'll take good care of her."

Lydia made a face. "You make me sound like a toddler you have to babysit. I knew your mama when she was your age, Lori Jane." She looked up at Shannon and Gideon. "Stay and have sandwiches with us, if you like."

Shannon saw something like horror on Gideon's face and stifled a laugh. "Actually, I promised my cousin I'd drop by to see a friend of his who runs a diner here in town. Gideon, you know your way around. Will you help me find Margo's Diner?"

"Sure," he said quickly, flashing her a grateful look. They waved goodbye to the women and headed back out to the street.

"You don't have to show me the way there," she said when they were alone again. "J.D. said once I find Sedge Road, I can't miss it."

He looked at her through narrowed eyes. "I don't mind showing you the way. I go there for lunch most days when I'm in town. It's about the only place left where you can get real home cooking."

She arched an eyebrow. "Are you asking me out to lunch?"

His brow furrowed with consternation. "No."

She laughed and slipped her hand into the crook of his elbow. "Come on, big guy. Let's go eat. No strings attached."

EVEN THOUGH MARGO'S Diner on Sedge Road was a hole in the wall, it was close enough to Terrebonne's three marinas to lure pleasure boaters who ventured into town in search of old-fashioned Southern home cooking. Gideon and Shannon reached the diner around eleven-thirty, after a quick but futile detour to Bay Pointe Marina in search of *Ahab's Folly*. They took a seat at the counter, where the proprietor, Margo, greeted Gideon with a welcoming smile and gave Shannon a curious, wary look.

"Wondered when you'd show up at my counter again, Gideon Stone." Margo pulled her order pad from her apron pocket. "Good timing, too. We got a mess of fresh-caught red snapper in just this morning. I know you like Harvey's blackened red snapper."

Harvey was the diner's curmudgeonly grill master. Not much personality but a genius touch on the grill.

"Sounds great—and I'll take a side of turnip greens and some of your vinegar slaw."

Margo handed Shannon a menu, glancing at Gideon as if she was waiting for an introduction. "Just let me know when you're ready to order, hon. Can I get you some sweet tea?"

"I'd love the biggest limeade you serve," Shannon answered with a friendly smile and a broad drawl that took the edge off Margo's wariness.

Gideon put Margo out of her misery. "Margo, this is Shannon Cooper. Shannon, this is Margo Shelby. Shannon's visiting Mrs. Ross," he explained vaguely.

"Pleased to meet you," Margo said with a genuine smile. "Cooper? You're not kin to Natalie Becker's new husband, are you?"

"As a matter of fact, that's why I'm here," Shannon replied. "My cousin J.D. told me to be sure to stop by and have lunch here before I left Terrebonne. He said to say hello and give you this." Shannon reached into her purse and pulled out a small photo wallet. Withdrawing a photograph, she handed it to Margo.

"Oh, my goodness, would you look at that!" She showed Gideon the photo.

It was a wedding photo of a tall, smiling man in his early forties in a black suit, standing next to a slim, red-haired bride Gideon recognized as Natalie Becker, former Chickasaw County Sheriff's Department deputy and oil money heiress.

"J.D. said to tell you thanks."

Margo laughed. "I don't think I had much to do with gettin' those two stubborn folks together, but I sure am glad to see 'em lookin' so happy."

Gideon watched as Shannon easily charmed Margo, who, like many small-town denizens, harbored a native suspicion of outsiders. One small wedding photo had been enough to convince her that Shannon was good people, however, and by the time Margo brought Shannon her order—turkey club sandwich, sweet potato fries and an enormous glass of iced limeade—the two women were chatting like old friends.

"I grew up by a big lake," Shannon commented as she unfolded a paper napkin and laid it across her lap. "My aunt and uncle own a marina there. But man, the size of some of the yachts I've seen at the marinas around here—they're bigger than houses! I guess people must live on them full-time or something."

"Some do, at least for the summer," Margo said with a nod. "A couple of summers ago, a gentleman from Naples—"

"Italy or Florida?" Shannon asked with a cheeky grin.

Margo laughed. "Florida. Retired stockbroker, or so he said. Took me out on a night cruise on his yacht before he headed back south. We didn't get out past Nightshade Island before I knew he was way outta my league, but mercy! It sure was nice livin' the dream a little while."

"I saw a gorgeous yacht at the Bay Pointe Marina the other day," Shannon said. She slanted a quick, warning look at Gideon. "I think it was called—dang, what was it? Something to do with Moby Dick—"

"Oh!" Margo's eyes lit up. "*Ahab's Folly,* I bet."

Gideon tried not to react. Shannon clapped her hands with delight. "Yes! *Ahab's Folly.* Nobody was around, but it was such a big, pretty boat, I have to admit to wishing I could've stowed away to see where it took me."

"Well, you'd have been surrounded by four big, good-lookin' fellas," Margo said with a wink. "They're fishing buddies from Galveston."

"Really? That doesn't look much like a fishing boat," Shannon said doubtfully. "I guess they could have taken that little dinghy out and fished, though." She shook her head, looking genuinely regretful. "I didn't see it when I was out there this morning. Too bad. Now that I know they're fishermen, I could've played off my mad fishing skills to finagle a ride!"

"They didn't say how long they'd be sticking around," Margo said. "But from what I hear, they've rented the boat slip through the end of the month, with an option to extend."

Gideon looked from Margo to Shannon, realizing that the little computer geek from Gossamer Ridge had just gotten more from Margo in a couple of minutes, without raising her suspicions, than he'd have been able to manage in an hour of subtle interrogation.

"I wonder why they named the yacht *Ahab's Folly,*" Shannon mused aloud. "Maybe one of them's a Melville fan?"

Melville, Gideon thought, a light flickering on.

"One of the fellows told me the boat used to belong to a former boss of theirs—he's the one who named it." Margo gave Shannon an apologetic look as the bell over the door rang again and new customers came in.

As Margo went to greet the newcomers, Gideon bent his head toward Shannon, speaking quietly. "Melville."

Her eyes narrowed slightly, then popped wide open. "Jackson Melville," she whispered back.

He nodded. Jackson Melville had been the CEO of Mac-Lear Security. He was currently awaiting trial in a federal penitentiary, having been deemed a flight risk and denied bail. But he might still be pulling strings from behind bars, especially if he had a lawyer willing to play go-between.

Margo came back to the counter after turning in the new orders. She poured more limeade for Shannon without asking and topped off Gideon's iced tea as well. "If you really want a ride on a yacht, we do have a few regular customers who own some of the bigger boats. I could probably arrange something."

"How do you know everything about everybody around here?" Shannon asked, sounding awed.

Margo smiled. "I just keep my ears open, darling."

"Did you catch the names of the men from *Ahab's Folly?*" Shannon asked. "I was just telling Gideon, I have some good friends from Galveston who are big into yachting. Wouldn't it be a hoot if the people from *Ahab's Folly* knew them?"

Gideon tried not to stare in awe. Shannon was good at this. Really good. She had a quick mind and a natural, disarming delivery of the most probing of questions. Why the hell hadn't Jesse Cooper put her out in the field before now?

"Well, I don't know any last names, but the big tall fellow with the quick temper's name is Craig, the good-lookin' devil with the blue eyes is Leo, the quiet black man is Damon and I believe the little fellow who needs a haircut is Ray."

Little fellow who needs a haircut... Gideon experienced a flash of memory, rocketing through his head so fast that he almost couldn't catch it. But he held on, forcing the image in his mind back to the surface.

Hard eyes, glittering with loathing. A feral grin as he braced himself for Gideon's reaction to being hit from behind. Sharp, narrow features that Gideon knew he'd seen before, although not with that long, floppy lock falling untidily over his hooded eyes.

Ray. Raymond.

Raymond Stephens.

He struggled not to react as Shannon and Margo continued chatting. His appetite fled completely, but he forced himself to keep eating, not wanting to attract Margo's attention by failing to eat half his lunch.

Raymond Stephens was a bitter blast from the past, one of the few fellow marines he'd ever met who had given him a bad case of the creeps. Wiry and fit, Stephens had been able to handle almost any physical task that Gideon, at that time a Special Operations training evaluator, had given the young marine to do.

But when it came to evaluation time, Gideon had given him low marks, based almost entirely on his conviction that Stephens was a risk to the Corps. Some marines, a very few, weren't emotionally or psychologically capable of the self-discipline necessary to temper violence with reason. Several incidents during training had convinced Gideon that Stephens was a war atrocity waiting to happen.

Stephens had washed out of Special Operations training, and he'd been livid. Threats, curses and finally a physical sneak attack on Gideon had led to the man's dishonorable discharge seven years ago.

Gideon had no idea where Stephens had gone after that. But given what he knew about MacLear Security's Special Services Unit, an ex-marine with good skills but no scruples might be exactly the kind of agent they were looking for.

Shannon finished her lunch and said her goodbyes to Margo in a tone that sounded genuinely regretful. Margo waved off her money when she tried to pay. "You brought me that pretty picture of J.D. and Natalie—I'm going to put it on my bulletin board out front and so many people in town will want to come see that Becker girl all gussied up and smiling, I'll probably double my business for a few weeks."

She took Gideon's money, however, and winked at him. "I like her. You should try to keep her around."

He just smiled and followed Shannon outside. "Your

brother is an idiot," he murmured once they were out on the sidewalk.

Shannon gave him a questioning look. "Beg your pardon?"

"You have no business being stuck in front of a computer all day. You're about as natural at interrogation as I've ever seen."

She smiled, looking ridiculously pleased by his assessment. "If I call Jesse, will you repeat that?"

He grinned at her, feeling a rush of heady satisfaction at being the person who made her look so happy. "Did your cousins really give you a photo to give to Margo?"

She shook her head. "They did tell me to stop by and see her while I was here, if I could, and let her know they got married. She apparently did a little matchmaking while J.D. was here. I just thought giving her the photo would make her more likely to open up."

"You're devious. I like that."

She chuckled. "They'll be happy I did. They just didn't think of it."

"Well, you did a good job getting information out of her. In fact, I think I know who one of the men is."

She looked at him, her expression suddenly hard to read. "Yeah?"

"The one Margo called Ray—I think he's an ex-marine I used to know. Raymond Stephens."

"You got all that from 'the fellow who needs a haircut is Raymond'?"

"You know how I told you I saw the man who attacked me at the marina the other day, but I couldn't quite remember him?"

"Yeah?"

"When she said his name," he said, "it clicked. I saw his face, clear as day. He isn't wearing his hair high and tight, of course, but those eyes—I'll never forget those eyes." He told her what he could remember about Raymond Stephens.

"Angry all the time. Sneaky, too. Vicious when cornered. And he held grudges. I told the major in charge of the training unit that Stephens was going to kill an innocent if we put him out there. A civilian or an ally, or maybe even another marine. So they washed him out."

Shannon's brow furrowed. "On your word?"

"Yeah, pretty much."

She shook her head. "And he holds grudges."

"Exactly." He dipped his head toward her, lowering his voice. "What if we're wrong about why they're trying to sneak onto Nightshade Island? Maybe it has nothing to do with General Ross's papers."

She looked up at him, her dark eyes scared. "You think maybe they're after you?"

"I hope they are," he admitted. "Then all I have to do is get as far away from here as I can and maybe Mrs. Ross won't feel as if she needs to leave her home."

Shannon frowned. "But Lydia had already decided to leave before any of this happened."

He had said more than he intended. Again. Her charms had worked on him as easily as on Margo at the diner. "Not exactly. There was an incident a couple of weeks ago. Up in Mobile. I'd dropped Mrs. Ross off at a furniture shop while I took the Caddy to a garage for a tune-up. When she left the furniture shop to go to a jewelry store across the street, she was mugged in broad daylight."

"Oh, no!"

"She fought them off, managed to hold on to her purse, but they pushed her down and scraped her up a little." He shook his head. "At the time, we thought it was just a random mugging, but—"

"But now you're not so sure."

"It was brazen. And until a couple of nights ago, odd."

"They were dressed in black with masks on?" Shannon guessed.

She really was spooky, Gideon thought. "Yeah. And they disappeared as soon as people came running to her rescue."

"That's why you didn't tell Lydia what the men on the island looked like."

"I think she guessed anyway," he said.

Shannon stopped walking and turned to look at him, emotion glowing in her dark eyes. She touched his chest again, her warm palm flattening against his sternum. "You're good to her. I know she's happy you're around."

He shook his head. "I'm a constant reminder of everything she's lost."

"No, you're a comfort." She smoothed her hand over his chest, her touch sparking a wildfire in his veins. The midday heat couldn't touch the inferno scorching his insides as he gazed at her upturned face, overwhelmed with the need to possess her, somehow, to brand her as his. It was an alien sensation, and frightening, but he was helpless against its power.

He lowered his head slowly. Deliberately. Giving her time to protest if she wanted to.

But she rose to her feet, curling her fingers in the fabric of his T-shirt. Closing the space between them, she brushed her mouth lightly against his.

He felt the world around them spinning into nothing, and it scared the hell out of him. As he started to pull away, she tightened her grip on his T-shirt and kept him close.

Their gazes locked. In her dark eyes, he saw an echo of the desire pounding in his own chest, and he was lost.

He bent his head again, his mouth slanting hard and hungry against hers. He sidestepped, pulling her with him until they had left the main sidewalk and slipped into the shadows of a narrow footpath between two buildings.

Salt air danced across his skin as she kissed him back, rising on her toes so she could wrap her arms around his neck. He dragged her against him, turning until her back flattened against the warm concrete block wall behind her. His mouth slid away from hers, moving down the curve of her jaw to nip lightly at the sensitive skin on the side of her neck.

"Get a room, geezers!" The voice, high-pitched and sarcastic, hit Gideon like a bucket of ice water. He stumbled backward, away from her, until his back flattened against the opposite wall.

A couple of teenaged boys ran away from the footpath, laughing wildly.

Shannon stared at him across the footpath, her eyes drunk with passion. She looked beautiful and vulnerable. So small. So fragile.

He'd walked away from their first kiss, not wanting to talk about it. And she'd let him.

He didn't think she would let him just walk away this time.

But to his surprise, she composed herself right in front of him, unhurried and giving a fine show of being unaffected. She straightened her blouse where his exploring hands had shifted it out of place and finger-combed her dark hair away from her face.

"Let's go find Lydia," she said, and walked out of the narrow alley, leaving him no choice but to follow.

Chapter Eleven

Lydia was in a happy mood at dinner that night, sharing tidbits of news she'd heard from her friends at the hair salon. To Shannon's eyes, she looked a decade younger. Maybe leaving the solitude of Nightshade Island would be good for her after all. At least Shannon hoped so.

As usual, she retired to her room early, leaving Shannon and Gideon to lock up for the night. Shannon put away the supper dishes while Gideon checked all the locks. Returning, he perched on one of the breakfast bar stools, watching as she put the last clean cup in the cabinet. "Looks like we're going to get some rain tonight."

"I thought the tropical storm was still a few days away."

"Only two now," he said. "And it's big enough that we'll see some feeder bands roll through tonight and tomorrow."

"You look worried."

"I can't shake what we talked about earlier. What if I'm the one bringing this mess raining down on Nightshade Island?"

"I don't think it's as simple as a grudge," she said with conviction, although she couldn't tell him the central reason she'd come to that conclusion, not without potentially putting someone in grave danger.

Gideon hadn't been the only person who'd recognized a name today.

"So you really think it's something in the general's collections?"

"I think we're on the right track, connecting those guys to MacLear. There are too many clues that add up—the Melville/*Ahab's Folly* connection, the commando-style infiltration of the island, AfterAssets's connection to Salvatore Beckett—"

He nodded. "I did think, once I remembered Ray Stephens, that he'd have been a prime prospect for the SSU. Skilled, physically brave and utterly lacking a moral compass. Fits the bill."

"So now we have to figure out what they want."

"Have you come across anything in the general's papers that raised any flags for you?" He sounded genuinely curious.

"Like what?"

"I'm not sure," Gideon admitted. "General Ross told me his suspicions about MacLear's possible involvement in Ford's death. But he also hinted the danger might not be over. He asked me to stick around to help him protect Mrs. Ross when he had to be away from the island."

Shannon leaned closer. "You think he was murdered, don't you?"

"The police can't say for sure that the crash wasn't an accident. It's just—the rate of speed the car was going when it crashed makes no sense. If anything General Ross was an overly cautious driver."

"Maybe he fell asleep and lost control?"

"Maybe, but not likely. He prided himself on his alertness."

She shook her head. "No tampering with the brakes?"

"The brake lines were intact, but that doesn't mean someone didn't bleed out the fluid of the brakes. There was almost no fluid in the chamber after the wreck, but the forensic mechanics couldn't be sure that didn't happen in the wreck itself—he drove into the bay, so any fluid from the cracked brake fluid chamber would have washed away."

"What would be the motive?"

Gideon glanced toward the stairs, as if worried about being overheard. He lowered his voice. "If the general knew something damaging to someone high in the food chain, which is definitely the impression I got, whoever's behind these intrusions could've burned Stafford House to the ground and not removed the threat as long as the general was alive."

A shudder of foreboding rippled up her spine. "So if we find whatever secret the general was hiding—"

"We could be targets, too."

She wondered if Jesse had any idea what he'd sent her into. She couldn't imagine he had; she'd been asking for a field case for over a year now with no luck, Jesse turning her down on cases far less dangerous than her trip to Nightshade Island was turning out to be.

"Maybe you should go home," Gideon said quietly.

She snapped her gaze up to his. "No."

"This isn't what you signed up for."

"No, but I'm capable of handling it," she said, wishing she sounded more confident. "I do have training, and you can't be here with Lydia twenty-four hours a day. But maybe we should bring more Coopers into this investigation."

She could see from Gideon's scowl that he wasn't crazy about the idea. "Calling in reinforcements may scare the bad guys off."

"And that would be a bad thing because?"

"Because maybe they decide to bide their time and go after Lydia and her treasures when neither of us are there to protect her."

"What's the alternative—luring the bad guys here?"

"No, but I don't want this to follow Lydia to her new home. It needs to end here and now."

He was calling Lydia by her first name regularly now, she noted. Coming to terms with actually feeling a connection to someone else? "Okay. I agree."

His expression softening, he laid his hand on her shoulder, his touch gentle. "I know this isn't what you expected when you came here. I'm sorry it's turned into such a mess."

"I'm glad I'm here. I want to help." She laid her palm against the center of his chest, knowing it would serve as a potent reminder of the kiss they'd shared earlier that day.

He gazed at her uncertainly, hunger blazing in his eyes. After a moment, he slid his hand around the back of her neck and tugged her to him, nuzzling his nose in her hair. "You make me crazy."

She couldn't hold back a smile, lifting her face to look up at him. "That doesn't have to be a bad thing."

He released her, his hand lingering at the base of her neck before dropping away, leaving her feeling bereft. "I've been thinking, if what the general knew was explosive enough to get him killed, maybe he wrote it down somewhere. Like, say, a coded journal."

"I might be able to find an e-book version of that cryptography book I have at home. It could help."

He nodded. "I'm going to go do my nightly patrol. Go get some rest. It's been a long couple of days. Lock up behind me."

She walked him to the door. "Be careful."

He managed a tired smile. "I always am."

After watching from the porch until he was out of sight, she went back inside, locked the door behind her and pulled out her cell phone. Climbing the stairs to her room, she called her brother.

Jesse sounded tired when he answered. "What's up, Shan?"

"A lot." She tamped down a sense of guilt at making the call to her brother behind Gideon's back. "But let's start with a question I've asked before. Why did you really send me here to Nightshade Island?"

There was such a long silence on Jesse's end of the line that Shannon wondered if she'd been disconnected. But he finally spoke. "Has something else happened?"

"Not in the last few hours. I'm more curious about why

you're not surprised that the SSU may be involved with whatever's going on here on Nightshade Island. I know Rick's told you about AfterAssets, hasn't he?"

"Yes."

"The connection to Salvatore Beckett and the timing of the company's creation don't give you pause?"

"Of course they do."

"Am I a sacrificial lamb here?"

"God, Shannon, what do you think I am?"

"A secretive bastard, for one thing," she snapped. "You sent me here knowing something was going on, but you didn't bother to tell me. Why?"

"Because I didn't want you overtly snooping around and getting into trouble."

"Why didn't you send Isabel or Rick or one of the other field operatives?"

He was quiet a moment before answering, "Nobody would suspect you of being a field operative."

Great. Just great.

"It's getting dangerous here. Gideon doesn't want me to call in the cavalry, but I thought I should at least give you the option."

Jesse's long pauses were beginning to unnerve her. When he didn't speak right away, she added, "What haven't you told me?"

Jesse released a long breath. "Remember Major Gantry?"

"The guy who turned state's evidence against Barton Reid?"

"Yeah. What I didn't tell you, or anyone outside of the family, is that shortly before Megan's wedding, there was another attempt on his life. He had to be moved immediately into witness security. But before he went, I got a chance to talk to him. And he told me that Barton Reid's not at the top of this conspiracy's totem pole. There's someone else. Gantry doesn't know who, but he says Reid and the other conspirators were deeply concerned about what three American generals knew."

Shannon's stomach tightened painfully. "Three generals?"

"We've come to the conclusion that the three generals in question almost certainly were the three generals in charge of the Kaziristan peacekeeping troops at the time of the insurrection." His voice deepened. "One of those three generals was Edward Ross."

Shannon pressed her hand over her mouth, feeling ill. Was Gideon right? Had General Ross's car crash not been an accident at all? "Wait a second," she said, something else occurring to her. "Wasn't Rita's father head of the Marine Corps troops in Kaziristan?"

"Yes, General Marsh is one of the three generals."

Baxter Marsh was the father of Jesse's former fiancée, Rita. Her younger sister had started working at Cooper Security earlier that summer, in Accounts Payable. Unlike Rita, who blamed Jesse for the breakup several years ago, Evie didn't seem to hold any grudges against the Coopers. "Have you talked to Evie about it?"

"I haven't yet, but I may have to now."

The grim tone of her brother's voice intensified the feeling of sick worry squirming in her belly. "What else aren't you telling me?"

"The third general in charge of the Kaziristan forces was Air Force General Emmett Harlowe."

"And?"

"This afternoon, he, his wife and his adult daughter were all reported missing."

Shannon sat down on her bed, troubled by the implications. "Someone's trying to get rid of the generals before they talk."

"That's certainly what it looks like," Jesse agreed. "Have you found anything in General Ross's papers that gave you pause?"

"Just one thing. And really, it might be nothing." She told

her brother about the coded journal. "It could have nothing to do with Kaziristan at all."

"Or it could have everything to do with it," Jesse said.

"I'm planning to download a digital version of that cryptography book I have at home if I can find one," she told Jesse. "I was going to try to get to work on it tomorrow morning."

"I'd rather you bring it home with you and do your detective work here," Jesse said.

She tightened her grip on the phone, not because she found her brother's suggestion outrageous, but because she found it so tempting. If he was right about the conspiracy swirling around the three generals, the danger to Lydia Ross—and by association, to her—might be far from over. After all, General Harlowe's whole family disappeared together.

Maybe these incursions by the men in black masks were attempts to silence Lydia Ross and take whatever potential evidence they could get their hands on. Maybe they had no intention of staying away, despite the temporary setback Gideon had dealt them.

Shannon wasn't a field operative. She'd never been involved in anything more dangerous than a nighttime hike up Fuller's Bluff on the east face of Gossamer Mountain.

But however light her experience in the field, Shannon did have skills that could lend an extra layer of protection for Lydia Ross and Nightshade Island. As long as she could help keep the wolves at bay, there was no way she could take the journal and run.

"I'd rather stay here," she said, swallowing her fear. "I can help Mrs. Ross." And Gideon, she added silently.

"Maybe I should come down there, then."

"Not yet," she said, remembering Gideon's earlier words. A full-force invasion of Coopers could easily deter the four intruders from having another go at the island, but Lydia Ross ultimately might be in more danger than ever. All they'd be doing was deferring the inevitable attack to a time and place where Lydia would be even more vulnerable. "Believe me, I'll call in the cavalry when it's necessary."

"Shannon—"

"Jesse, you sent me here. Now you're just going to have to trust me to handle the situation you sent me into. Okay?"

There was a thick pause on the other end of the line before Jesse said, "Okay, but stay in touch."

"I will." She said goodbye to her brother and hung up the phone, her mind already moving several steps ahead.

Jesse hadn't said outright to keep the information about the three generals to herself, but he'd certainly implied that the information was hush-hush. So was it something she could share with Gideon or not?

Yes. Gideon had a right to know what they might be up against.

She went out the French doors on the balcony side of her room, hoping to spot Gideon on his nightly island patrol. He was nowhere in sight, but the mild salt breeze coming off the Gulf of Mexico lifted her hair and filled her lungs, leaving her unwilling to confine herself to her room just yet. The silvery moon struggled to cast its light through the dark clouds scudding across the sky, the first hint of the coming tropical storm.

It would be raining by morning, she thought. Would that help or hinder their efforts to protect Nightshade Island?

Seeing no sign of Gideon from her side of the house, she circled around to where she had a good view of both the caretaker's house behind the garden and, several yards farther toward the beach, the stark silhouette of Nightshade Island Lighthouse.

The caretaker's house was dark, she saw. But in the lighthouse, a light flickered up top in the service room.

Gideon must have gone up to check the lighthouse, she realized, already heading back to her room. She tugged on a pair of sneakers, went downstairs and let herself out through the garden door.

GIDEON WALKED SLOWLY along Nightshade Island's sandy eastern shore, trying to concentrate. He was out here to search for any signs of intruders—unexpected movements in the gloom, out-of-place sounds—but his mind kept wandering back to Terrebonne and the feel of Shannon Cooper's lips beneath his own.

He was a long way from boyhood. He'd known a lot of women, cared deeply for one or two in his younger days, but none of them had crawled under his skin and put down roots the way Shannon Cooper had in the space of three short days. He actually felt a strange, physical withdrawal from her presence that made him feel incomplete.

The sensation was disturbing and highly distracting, and he'd damn well better figure out a way to make it stop before he did something that could destroy them both.

He could feel the blackness inside him. Anger. Hurt. Resentment. And a terrible fear that his father's words were true. *"You're just like me."*

He'd had people tell him what he felt was normal, but he couldn't believe it was really true. Not after seeing in his father's depravity what that kind of blackness could do to a man's soul.

How it could destroy everything—and everyone—around him.

Shannon Cooper didn't need the darkness of Gideon's world encroaching on hers. So he had to stop thinking about her. Stop wanting her.

He had to figure out a way to protect her from not only the dangers posed by the intruders but also from himself.

The moon had ducked behind a dark cloud, pitching the island into deep night before Gideon could make out more than a slender shape moving through the tall sea grass. But a glimpse was all he needed to recognize Shannon Cooper.

And she was heading for the lighthouse.

Don't follow her, commanded a voice in the back of his

head. But it seemed a whisper compared to the raging of his blood in his veins.

Drawn by a force too primal to resist, he angled across the beach and headed up the shallow rise to higher ground, hating himself with every step but powerless to stop.

"GIDEON?" SHANNON FLASHED her light up to the top of the lighthouse, where the spiral stairway ended in a narrow landing just outside the service room. The beam of light, filtered through the lacy ironwork of the metal stairs, painted delicate, undulating shadows across the dank stone walls.

No answer came from above, although she thought she heard soft sounds of movement at the top of the lighthouse. A shuffle of footsteps echoed through the cylindrical space, as if Gideon was moving in the darkness just beyond the reach of her flashlight.

Odd, she thought. If she could hear Gideon moving around above, why hadn't he heard her calling him? She was almost halfway to the top when she realized she might not be hearing Gideon above at all.

She might be hearing one of the intruders.

Instinctively, she reached for the weapon that should have been tucked in a holster on her hip. But she'd left the GLOCK back at Stafford House, feeling safe—with Gideon out here, keeping watch—to venture out unarmed.

Stupid!

Snapping off the flashlight, she reversed course as quietly as possible, moving backward slowly, keeping one hand on the stair railing and her eyes straining to see any sign of movement in the gloomy void above. She'd descended only a few feet when she heard another, less furtive sound than the whispery noises she'd heard earlier. Footsteps, she realized, moving rapidly on the stairs.

Coming from below.

Her heart danced wildly in her chest as she froze, uncertain which direction to go. Her hand closed around the flashlight, her fingertip trembling on the switch. One click of the light and she could be certain who was coming up the lighthouse stairs.

But she'd also reveal her own position, making herself an easy target.

Up, she decided. She could get to the service room and set off the foghorn. That would bring Gideon running for Stafford House and she could call out to him from the catwalk.

She scooted up the stairs as fast as she could, not bothering with stealth. Speed was more important. She had to set off the horn before whoever was coming up the steps from below could stop her.

She hit the narrow concrete landing outside the service room and skidded to a stop, nearly slamming face-first into the door. She pushed it open, slipped inside and closed the door behind her. Her heart pounding, she flicked on the light, swinging it in an arc around the service room, trying to regain her bearings.

For a second, the figure in the corner didn't register. Her flashlight beam swept past it before the image clicked in her brain.

She swung the flashlight back, catching the black-clad figure moving with catlike speed. She jerked back, her hand slamming into the door. The flashlight clattered to the floor, the light disappearing.

In the sudden, shocking darkness, the intruder grabbed her, his hand flattening over her mouth. His low voice rumbled against her like thunder.

"Not a word, Shannon. Not one word."

Chapter Twelve

The voice was familiar. Barely.

There was a snick, and light came on in the service room again, brighter than her small light. The grip holding her in place loosened and she made her move, shooting toward the door.

He grabbed her again. "Shannon, it's Damon North."

She twisted around to face the intruder. He let go of her with one hand and flashed the light on his face.

Dark, intelligent eyes shined from a handsome brown face. She'd seen him only once before, nearly six months earlier, but Damon North was unforgettable.

"I knew it!" she whispered. "When Margo said that one of the four men from the yacht was named Damon—"

"There's someone coming up the stairs," he whispered. "I have to go outside. You have to cover for me."

"Why should I do that? What the hell are you doing with those guys?"

"You know what I'm doing. The same thing I've been doing for years." He didn't argue further, slipping out the side door and escaping onto the narrow catwalk outside. The light from his flashlight shut off, plunging her into inky blackness again.

She barely had time to reorient herself to the dark when

the door from the stairway opened and someone burst inside, coming in low and fast.

"Don't move!" he commanded in an authoritative growl. The familiar voice was a comforting relief.

"Gideon," she breathed.

His flashlight snapped on, stabbing her eyes with its bright beam. "Why did you run?"

"I didn't know it was you," she shot back, her nerves still humming with high voltage.

"I thought you were running from someone else."

She released a weak, nervous laugh, thinking about the man out on the catwalk and wondering why she wasn't telling Gideon all about him. Had she lost her mind?

Aloud, she said, "This whole mess has us all on edge."

Gideon nodded, moving closer. "You okay?"

Tell him about Damon. Tell him now.

"I'm fine." She opened her mouth to tell him about Damon, but suddenly the foghorn sounded, a low-pitched howl of distress.

"Lydia," Gideon breathed.

Shannon's heart skipped a beat. "Are you sure it's not a trap?"

"It doesn't matter," Gideon said, already racing for the stairs.

Shannon started to head down behind him, but the sound of the door from the catwalk sliding open stopped her in her tracks.

As Gideon's footsteps grew even farther away, she whirled around to face Damon, who had slipped back inside the service room.

"Are your people here? Is that why Lydia sounded the horn?"

His lip curled. "They're not my people. You know that."

"I'm not sure I know anything about you at all."

"I helped your sister-in-law."

"You nearly got her killed," she shot back. "And you put my cousin's baby in danger with your stupid undercover games."

"The SSU hasn't disbanded. You know that as well as anyone. I have to cut them out at the root."

"And you're willing to risk the life of an innocent woman like Lydia Ross?" She should have told Gideon. Let Damon see if he could talk him into trust and leniency. "I have to go—Gideon might need me."

"It's not them," Damon said with confidence. "I need to talk to you."

"Not now," she said flatly, turning and striding out to the stairs.

"Leave your balcony door open," he called softly after her.

She made her way down as quickly as she could, hampered by the utter lack of light. But she made it to the ground without incident and hurried out into the fresh air.

A light rain had begun falling while she was inside the lighthouse, and as she dashed across the uneven ground toward Stafford House, she heard the growing restlessness of the Gulf, swelling waves slapping against the shoreline with increased agitation.

The storm was on its way.

By the time she reached Stafford House, the foghorn had stopped wailing. She dashed through the French doors and found Lydia sitting on the sofa, looking sheepish and a little bit frail.

"Are you okay?" Shannon asked, hurrying to her side. Gideon sat on the coffee table in front of Lydia, his expression hard to read.

"I'm fine," Lydia said with an embarrassed grimace. "I had a thought about Edward's journal and I went to your room to look for you, but I didn't see you. And then, when I looked out on the balcony for you, I saw lights in the lighthouse and, well, I guess I overreacted."

Shannon caught Lydia's hands between her own. "We're all on edge."

"No harm done," Gideon said in a gentle rumble.

"Where did you go?" Lydia asked.

"I saw Shannon heading to the lighthouse, so I went to see where she was going." Gideon spoke when Shannon didn't answer right away. His blue eyes turned to her. "What were you doing up there?"

Now, she thought. *Now's the time to tell him about Damon.*

But a memory flashed through her mind, something her brother Rick had said a few months earlier, when Damon North's plan to smoke out some SSU assassins had gone badly wrong, putting her brother and the woman who was now his wife in deadly danger.

"Undercover is hell," he'd said flatly when Shannon and the rest of the family had expressed outrage at Damon's actions. "He lives every day as someone he's not, and he knows that breaking that cover for a moment could mean his death. He has control over little, but he's got the guts to go out there and take a risk for a good reason. I'm not going to second-guess him."

Even Amanda, the target of the SSU goons Damon had been trying to bring down, had agreed with Rick. "I've been in that same place. You can't make everything come out right. Undercover operatives play cynical, wretched games with some of the baddest bad guys there are, because it's the only way to get on the inside and stay there long enough to do the job. It's something you can't understand unless you've been there."

Damon had asked for her silence. She could give it to him, at least until she heard him out.

Shannon pasted on a smile. "I thought I saw you moving around up in the lighthouse, so I went to look."

That much, at least, was the truth, and it was easy enough to tell without flinching.

"Wasn't me," Gideon said thoughtfully.

"It was probably my imagination," she said with a self-conscious smile. She turned her attention back to Lydia. "You said you had a thought about the general's journal?"

"Well, two thoughts, actually. Or, really, two people. My husband spent a lot of time during the last days of his life conferring with a couple of old military friends. Generals he'd served with on his last tour before his retirement."

Shannon's skin prickled, remembering the reason she'd gone to the lighthouse in the first place. She wanted to tell Gideon about the three generals, but her encounter with Damon North had upturned her world.

"You think one of them might know how to break the code?" Gideon asked.

"I think it would have to be both of them," Lydia said. "Before Edward died, he told me about a way the field commanders sent top-secret coded messages to them—the cryptographers devised a multipart code that required input from all the parties involved to completely decrypt the message. It sounded hopelessly complicated to me, but apparently with the problem of underlings passing information to those internet leakers—"

"They'd want a code that only they would understand between them," Gideon said with a grim nod.

"So you think to break the code in the journal, we might have to contact the other two generals," Shannon said, her heart sinking.

"It makes sense," Gideon said. "The other two generals—Harlowe and Marsh, right?" He looked at Shannon, adding for her benefit, "Those were the other two top men heading the Kaziristan peacekeeping mission."

"I know," she said bleakly. "And there's something you should know."

Both Gideon and Lydia looked at her, concern in their eyes at the troubled tone of her voice.

"I talked to my brother earlier this evening." Shannon looked at Gideon. "It's why I went looking for you at the lighthouse. But first, I have to tell you about something that happened back in the spring."

It had all started with an attempted assassination. "My brother Rick's wife, Amanda, is a former CIA agent. And the reconstituted group of mercenaries who used to work for MacLear Security were sent by Barton Reid to kill her because of something she knew."

Lydia lifted one hand to her mouth, her eyes widening.

"Amanda had been captured by al-Adar rebels in Kaziristan a few years ago. She'd seen the face of a rebel leader and could identify him."

"Khalid Mazir," Gideon growled.

"Yes." Shannon looked at him. "They kept Amanda's name out of the papers when that mess went down, but she was the informant who identified him as an al-Adar operative."

"Your sister-in-law put Barton Reid back in jail," Lydia said with growing understanding. "Well, good for her. Never cared for the slimy old bastard in the first place."

Shannon smiled at Lydia's unfiltered words. "No argument from me."

"What does this have to do with the three generals?" Gideon asked.

"That's another twist in the story." She looked at Lydia. "My sister Megan was married to a soldier who died in Kaziristan four years ago. We've recently learned that MacLear SSU agents were behind his death—Vince had begun asking inconvenient questions about some things he'd seen Barton Reid doing in Kaziristan. He told the wrong person in his chain of command, apparently, and ended up dying for his effort."

"My God." Lydia's hand flew to her mouth again.

"We didn't know he was murdered at the time. We assumed it was a combat death. But last spring, my sister finally learned the truth, although she nearly got killed for it, too."

Gideon shook his head. "Your family seems to be made up of trouble magnets."

"Sometimes, when you try to do the right thing, that's what happens." Lydia reached out to touch Shannon's hand. "Your sister must have been devastated to learn how her husband died."

"She was, but it was better to know the truth." Shannon took a deep breath, aware that she was about to deliver a similarly devastating bit of news to Lydia about her own husband's death.

Gideon's hand closed over her arm, drawing her gaze to his face. She saw his troubled thoughts shining from his blue eyes. He might not know exactly what she was about to say, but he clearly knew it had something to do with his own suspicions about General Ross's death.

She held his gaze, her chin up. Lydia had to know the truth, even if it was painful. "You may have heard about a new witness in the Barton Reid case. He was an army captain who had helped cover up my brother-in-law's murder. He'd been blackmailed into it and finally turned state's evidence. He ended up going into witness protection."

Gideon nodded, as if he'd heard at least part of the story before, but Lydia looked surprised. "I knew Barton Reid had been indicted again," she said quietly, "but all this horror about murdered soldiers—"

"My brother talked to the witness right before he went into witness security. The captain gave him a new piece of information about the case against Reid. It seems the captain overheard Barton Reid talking about the trouble he was having with three generals."

Lydia straightened suddenly.

"The implication," Shannon added slowly, "was that the

generals may have known too much about what Reid was doing. They were trouble."

Lydia looked stricken.

Shannon reached across, placing her hand over Lydia's trembling hands. "I'm sorry. There's really no easy way to say this—"

"Shannon—" Gideon's voice was low and strangled.

"Let her talk," Lydia said quietly, turning her hands to clasp Shannon's.

"My brother believes your husband's crash wasn't an accident."

"He can't know that," Gideon said harshly.

Shannon turned to look at him. "Maybe not, but here's what we do know. A couple of days ago, General Emmett Harlowe, his wife and his adult daughter were all reported missing."

ONE OF THESE days, all the sleep he was missing was going to catch up with him, Gideon thought as he hung up the phone and leaned back against the soft cushions of Lydia Ross's sofa. Lydia had gone to bed, and Shannon was up in her room, trying to catch a few hours of sleep before morning, but he'd been on the phone with old friends from his Marine Corps days who were now working as civilian cops in Georgia, where the Harlowe family had disappeared.

The facts were sparse on the ground. From what his buddies could tell him, General Harlowe, his wife, Catherine, and their daughter, Annie, made the trip to Pea Hollow, Georgia, where Mrs. Harlowe's family had owned a small fishing cabin for generations. It had been Mrs. Harlowe's sister who'd arrived for a planned visit earlier that day and found the place in shambles and all three of the Harlowes missing.

"There was blood," Mitch Sweeney had told Gideon, his voice grim over the telephone line.

"How much?"

"Enough to be worrisome," Sweeney had admitted. "Just got off the phone with one of the local deputies who investigated. He thinks it's possible one or more could be bodily hurt. And here's another nasty thought—nobody's actually seen them for about five days. They may have been missing since the day after they arrived."

Sweeney hadn't been able to add much more, but what he'd told Gideon was enough to send his mind swirling. He'd been suspicious for a while about the general's car crash, but to hear Shannon speak his nebulous thoughts aloud, tying them to a conspiracy that could very well run deep and wide through a large swath of the U.S. government—

From outside, a soft scraping sound drew his attention. He listened carefully, but it didn't repeat.

Quietly, he stood and went to the front door, peering through the narrow glass inset at the top of the door. Outside, all looked quiet, although the Gulf was churning even more than it had been earlier that evening when he'd been out on patrol.

Lydia had plans to meet a friend for lunch tomorrow—today, he amended with a quick glance at his watch. It might be the last day they'd be able to take the boat out safely before the tropical storm hit.

Maybe he should insist Lydia stay on the mainland. They could all move into a motel in Terrebonne, or even drive up to Mobile where there would be safety in numbers. It would leave the island unprotected, but he had a feeling that the coded journal Shannon had found was almost certainly the item the intruders were looking for.

He wondered how they knew about the book. And why they hadn't looked for it before now.

Nobody's seen them for five days. Mitch Sweeney's words flickered through his mind.

Emmett Harlowe surely knew about General Ross's journal, didn't he? He'd have to know to help decode it should the time come to do so.

If the SSU had somehow gotten their hands on the Harlowes, maybe used the general's wife or daughter as leverage, would he have spilled what he knew about the journal? As secrets went, it wouldn't have been a hard choice, he supposed. The coded journal would be useless without input from Harlowe and the third general, crusty old Baxter Marsh.

He would make more calls in the morning, he decided. See if he could get in touch with General Marsh.

As he started toward the kitchen to turn out the lights, he heard the same furtive scuffling sound he'd heard before. But this time, it hadn't come from outside.

It was somewhere in the house.

WHEN THE FRENCH doors from the balcony outside Shannon's room opened silently, she wasn't exactly surprised. She'd left the door open, as Damon North had asked. But seeing his dark shape glide almost noiselessly into her bedroom still made her heart skip a beat.

She turned on the bedside lamp, illuminating his tall, lean form.

"Turn off the light," he commanded softly.

"You don't give the orders around here," she answered flatly.

"Please."

With a sigh, she turned off the lamp, plunging the room back into inky midnight. "You're a fool to come here tonight. Gideon Stone is right downstairs. If he hears you—"

"Just shut up and listen."

Shannon clamped her mouth into a line of pure annoyance, but she let him speak uninterrupted.

"I'm undercover. Believe it or not, the business with your sister-in-law last spring got me back in, even though the SSU operation was a bust."

"Congratulations."

The mattress shifted beneath her, and she made out the dark, amorphous shape of him at the end of her bed. "I don't know how much you know—"

"Why don't you tell me what I don't know," she answered guardedly.

"There's something in this house that the SSU wants."

"What is it?"

"A journal. Information has come into our—" He paused, making a noise of frustration. "Into *their* hands. They know General Ross kept a coded journal regarding some of the things that were going on in Kaziristan a few years ago. Something that is probably still going on today, if not in Kaziristan, then in other hot spots around the globe."

"What kind of conspiracy?" From her family's experiences with the SSU, she knew there must be some sort of global power-grab going on, but so far, even government investigators weren't sure how far the corruption went or just how ambitious it might be.

Damon didn't answer right away. Shannon wondered if his silence indicated dangerous knowledge—or frustrated ignorance.

The latter, as it turned out. "That's one secret I haven't been given access to," he admitted. "I don't know if any of my current crew knows."

"Just in it for the money?"

"A big motivator," Damon agreed. "But I think one of the crew may want something a little more personal out of this."

"Revenge on Gideon Stone?" she suggested.

"You already know?"

"Gideon recognized one of the people who knocked him out and kicked him while he was down." Her gut tightened with anger. "You weren't in on that, were you?"

"No. I've been here on the island for days. I was in the lighthouse the first night, when you set off the horn. Five of us made it ashore that night. Four came in the Zodiac. I swam ashore on the lighthouse side of the island and stayed when the others left."

Shannon remembered that first night at the lighthouse, when she'd had a strong feeling someone was watching. She'd felt the same thing later, the day she went to find her penlight and ended up in the service room again, fighting the feeling she wasn't alone. "You were hiding in the lighthouse the whole time?"

"You nearly caught me twice." He stood and paced quietly to the window, his shoes barely making a sound on the hardwood floor. "I decided the third time, I should just tell you I was there and see if you'd be willing to help."

"How did you know it was me? We barely met last spring—"

"I sneaked into the house and searched the upstairs rooms," Damon admitted. "When I found your ID and realized you were a Cooper—one of *those* Coopers—"

"What do you want me to do?" she asked warily.

"Find the general's journal and give it to me," he answered.

Chapter Thirteen

"Are you crazy?" Shannon's outraged voice carried from behind her closed door, making Gideon pause in mid-stride. If she was still up, that might have been what he'd heard. Probably talking to her brother on the phone, he realized, and started to reverse course back down the stairs to the main floor.

Then he heard the second voice. Low. Well-modulated. A man's voice. And it definitely wasn't coming over any phone line.

"I'm on your side. I don't want that journal getting into the hands of the SSU, either."

"For all intents and purposes, you *are* the SSU," Shannon said flatly. "What makes you think you can keep the journal out of their hands?"

Gideon padded silently to the door of the blue bedroom, anger rising like fire in his chest. What the hell did she think she was doing? Had she let an intruder willingly into her room? She didn't sound scared, only frustrated and distrustful.

What kind of game was she playing?

A tiny part of him argued for biding his time, letting her play out whatever she was trying to do. Shannon had proved herself so far, putting herself in danger to protect Lydia when the intruders came. She'd also helped him when he'd staggered home after a beating.

Or had it all been an act on her part, a plan to worm her way into Lydia's inner circle?

Think about what she said. She just said she doesn't want the SSU to have the journal.

"I can get it decrypted. Can you?" the man countered, a hint of cocky confidence in his tone.

"What if I can?"

"You have the key?"

"What if I do?"

The man let out a low growl of frustration. "This isn't a game, Shannon. You know that. You've nearly lost family members to these people. Why are you fighting me?"

"Because my brother sent me here to do a job, and I trust him a hell of a lot more than I trust you," Shannon snapped. "I heard you out. I'm glad you're out there keeping an eye on those heartless bastards, but I'm not going to let you manipulate me into betraying people I promised to help."

Gideon had heard enough. He opened the door.

He got a glimpse of an African-American man, dressed entirely in black. The flash of a compact pistol barrel rising to bear down on him. He heard Shannon's soft intake of breath.

Gideon ducked and rolled, coming up with the Walther out.

But Shannon stood between him and the man in black.

"Get out of the way, Shannon," he growled.

"Gideon, you don't understand—"

"Move out of the way."

"Listen to her, man." The man in black did the one thing Gideon did not expect.

He lowered his weapon.

"Gideon, this is not an SSU operative," Shannon said slowly, raising her hands toward him. He realized he was still holding his Walther in shooting position.

"Give your weapon to Shannon, butt first," he told the intruder.

"That's really not necessary," Shannon protested.

"Take the weapon, Shannon," Gideon snapped. "If you want me to put down my weapon, take his."

She released a short huff of breath and took the SIG SAUER P229 from the intruder's outstretched hand.

"Come over here," he said.

Shannon shook her head. "I'm not going to let you shoot him."

Gideon glared at her. "Do you think I'm going to shoot an unarmed man? Really?" Although, as angry as he felt at the moment, he wasn't sure he could blame her for wondering.

She closed her eyes for a second, as if to shut them both out of her mind. Then she opened her eyes and crossed slowly to his side, standing a little out of his reach.

Stunned by a sudden, powerful urge to drop his weapon and pull her into his arms, Gideon forced his gaze back to the man standing across the room, his back to the open French doors. "Name?" he asked.

"I go by Damon North," the black man answered smoothly. "That's all you'll get from me, so take it and move on."

"Who do you work for?"

"A company named Chimera Security."

"Never heard of it."

"You're not supposed to have."

"What do you want here?" Gideon asked.

The man's dark eyes slanted toward Shannon. "I'm here to stop the newly reconstituted Special Services Unit, formerly of MacLear Security, from destroying evidence that could take down dangerous elements within the U.S. government."

"Looks to me like you're just another thug trying to jerk people around."

"Looks can be deceiving."

Gideon bit back a growl. "Any more clichés you want to toss my way before you tell me what you really want?"

A flare of anger blazed in Damon's eyes. "I'm deep undercover, trying to thwart people who want a journal written by Edward Ross. They're willing to kill everyone on this island to get it, if that's what it takes. Believe me, I'm putting my neck on the line to keep that from happening. I've fought them every inch of the way. So don't get in my way."

"Leave. Tell your friends there's nothing here. And don't come back."

Damon's nostrils flared, the only sign of anger he showed. The sign of a professional.

The thought gave Gideon little comfort.

"Three days ago, a black ops unit kidnapped General Emmett Harlowe, his wife, Cathy, and his daughter, Annie, from a cabin in the north Georgia woods," Damon said flatly. "They used the general's wife and daughter to get information from the general—information about a journal that he and two other generals compiled to document a high-level conspiracy between agents of the U.S. government and criminal and terrorist elements around the globe. I know this because the cell I infiltrated was ordered three days ago to retrieve this journal and destroy it."

Gideon's gut tightened. Had this man overheard his earlier conversation with Lydia and Shannon? Or had he known beforehand?

The timing of the attempted invasion of the island seemed to correspond to what little they knew about the Harlowes' abduction. But their nocturnal visitor could have heard the story on the radio anytime during the day. If Gideon had run the radio in the Caddy that day while they drove through town, he might have heard the news as well.

He looked at Shannon and found her gaze locked on him,

her eyes wide and dark with anxiety. "Why did you let him in here?"

"She knows me," Damon answered for her.

"Damon helped my cousin stop a drug cartel seeking vengeance on him for something he did in the marines. And back in March, he helped my sister-in-law escape SSU assassins." Her gaze slanted toward Damon. "Sort of. Didn't exactly work how it was supposed to."

"I almost got shot luring them away from Amanda," Damon said. "I don't want the SSU to win. We're on the same side."

"I'm on the side that has no intention of letting you manipulate us into giving you anything," Gideon said.

Shannon turned to Damon. "Are the Harlowes still alive?"

Damon gave her an odd look. "I don't know. Nobody's said. My guess is, at least the general is still alive. They won't want to kill him before they get their hands on the journal."

Shannon turned to look at Gideon. She didn't say it aloud, not in front of Damon, but he knew what she was thinking. The kidnapping of Emmett Harlowe and his family raised the stakes exponentially and made protecting Lydia that much harder for them.

He looked at Damon. "I suggest you go."

"Can I have my SIG?"

"Shannon, empty the mag and the chamber and give it back."

She shot him an exasperated look but did as he asked. "He probably has ammunition hidden elsewhere."

"And he can go find it as soon as he gets the hell out of this house."

Shannon handed Damon the empty SIG. "Get off the island."

"I can't. I was stationed here for a purpose."

"To steal the journal?" Gideon asked.

"To kidnap Lydia Ross."

SHANNON stepped quickly between Gideon and Damon, her hand closing over Gideon's gun hand as he lifted the weapon on instinct. "Don't be rash, Gideon. Please."

Gideon glared past her to Damon, barely leashed violence burning in his eyes. "You heard what he said."

"I said I was stationed here for that purpose." Damon's reasonable tone did little to dim the fire in Gideon's gaze. "I didn't say it was my intention."

"You said it to goad him," Shannon snapped back at him. "Shut up unless you can be straight with us without the super-spy dog-and-pony show."

"You should have told me about him as soon as we were out of the lighthouse," Gideon said flatly, turning his dark gaze on her. "I thought you were playing things straight."

She tightened her grip on his arm. "I had to hear what Damon had to say, and I couldn't let you go off half-cocked before he got the chance."

In the blue depths of his eyes, she saw an unexpected flare of pain. "I guess I can't blame you for that. I mean, I'm just the hot-headed hired muscle, right?"

"No!" she denied swiftly, but she could see how her actions might have indicated otherwise. She lowered her voice. "I know how much you care about Lydia. You would do anything to protect her. You're not going to take any chances with her safety on anyone's word."

"I'd take *your* word," he protested, but she didn't hear real conviction behind his declaration.

"No, you wouldn't." She tried not to let her own hurt show. "You've known me three days and there's a lot at stake."

"As riveting as all this personal drama may be," Damon drawled, "there's still the matter of four very dangerous men who want that journal."

"We don't even know there is a journal," Shannon said, gazing up at Gideon. His gaze softened a hint.

"There's a journal," Damon said darkly. "A damn fine air force general sacrificed his soul admitting to its existence."

Shannon's gut tightened. "Tell them you searched and it's not here."

"They won't believe me."

"*Make* them believe you."

"It doesn't work that way," Gideon said softly. "We have to find the journal and decode it." He spoke to her silently with his gaze.

"Good luck with that," Damon said.

Gideon's gaze shot across the room. "I suppose you could do better?"

"I have assets you don't."

"Such as?"

"You know I can't tell you."

Shannon flattened her hand against Gideon's chest, trying to soothe the fierce energy she felt radiating from him like waves of heat. "This will get us nowhere, Gideon. Maybe we should at least listen to what he has to say."

Gideon flattened his hand on top of hers. He looked down at her for a long moment, as if anchoring himself in her gaze, then looked back at Damon. "Five minutes."

"I can do it in two," Damon said, and proceeded to talk.

GIDEON SLEPT THAT night only because he knew he had to be in top form the next day. Everything was at stake. Lydia's life, Shannon's, his own—and if all the facts they'd gathered over the past few days were true, the security of the United States and its allies might well hinge on what General Ross's journal might reveal. So he stayed the night at Stafford House, in the spare bedroom next door to Shannon's, trusting his internal alarm, honed by over a decade of high-intensity combat situations, to keep the inhabitants of the island from coming to any harm.

Waking around 5:00 a.m., he watched the sunrise from the

balcony outside Shannon's room after reassuring himself that both of his charges had made it through the night unharmed.

The waters of the Gulf churned with restless energy, the whitecaps, whipped up by the coming tropical storm, larger and more powerful than usual, but nothing yet that would make a trip to the mainland inadvisable.

Damon had gone away empty-handed the night before. Neither Shannon nor Gideon himself had let on that they already knew the location of the coded journal. He hoped Damon had bought the story, at least for now. There were parts of the man's outlined plan that Gideon was willing to take a risk on—with precautions added from his end—but the safety of the journal wasn't one of them. As a marine, he understood that some things were more important than life itself.

The journal might well be one of those things.

The door behind him opened, and he smelled the sweet, sleepy scent of Shannon before he saw her. "Good morning," he murmured.

She settled next to him at the railing, her dark-eyed gaze on the rain clouds gathering in the south. "Is it?"

"For the moment." He turned to look at her fully. "Did you get some sleep?"

"Yeah. Bad dreams, though."

He could sympathize. His own sleep had been marred by anxious nightmares that he couldn't remember but couldn't quite shake.

"Are we doing the right thing?" she asked.

She'd been the one most willing to hear Damon out the night before, but whatever she'd dreamed seemed to have shaken her confidence in the plan. His own gut tightened with worry, now that she was beginning to second-guess what they'd agreed to do the night before.

"We have to get Lydia safely away from here and put her somewhere nobody will go after her," he said after a long pause in which he played out the options in his mind, coming to the same conclusion he'd come to the night before. "At least for a day or two. If Damon's buddies think she's been kidnapped, according to plan, they won't go looking for her. They'll think he's got her safely tucked away as leverage against me."

"Against us," Shannon corrected.

"You're collateral, too, Shannon. I can't play this out if I'm worried about you. You need to go home for real, not just for show."

Her brow furrowed with dismay. "I suppose you'd tell a fellow marine to leave the battlefield so you wouldn't have to worry about his getting shot? How many times did you try that before you were knocked flat on your butt, Lieutenant Stone?"

"None," he admitted, hating that she was right. Whether he liked it or not, she was an asset, not a liability, just as his fellow marines had been.

The difference was, he'd never wanted to kiss any of them. And right now, all he wanted to do was kiss Shannon Cooper until they both forgot there was a world outside.

That was the distraction. Not a lack of trust in her ability—he'd seen her in action. Clearly she was strong, capable and well-trained.

But if she got hurt in the middle of this mess—

"Please don't treat me like I'm useless," she said softly, dropping her gaze in frustration. "Don't treat me like a fragile thing that has to be wrapped in cotton and hidden safely away."

He had a strong feeling her words had deeper meaning than just their current situation. He couldn't let himself hear beyond the surface, however. "I know you're not useless. You're definitely an asset to this situation. But you're going to have to forgive me if I wish you'd sit it out where you won't get hurt."

"I don't think I could sit it out, even if I thought it was for the best." She lifted her small, strong hand and planted it in the center of his chest. "Not if you're in the middle of the fight."

Her words made him ache as much as her touch made him burn. He couldn't afford to feel so much for her. For anyone. He might be known as fierce in battle, perhaps even reckless where his own safety was concerned, and he couldn't really argue against such a characterization, but he'd always guarded his emotions. Fear of that darkness inside him from birth, his father's grim legacy, had set him adrift emotionally. Getting close to other people—letting them get close to him—seemed a far more daunting prospect than running through a battle zone with shells and bullets raining around him.

Heat seemed to radiate from that small point of contact beneath Shannon's palm, spreading through him like strength. As he'd done last night, he laid his hand over hers, sliding his thumb over her knuckles. He had meant to simply remove her hand and let it go, but instead, he lifted her fingers to his mouth and touched his lips to them.

She lifted her other hand and touched his jaw, her fingers sliding over his overnight growth of beard, making a rasping noise. "I'm scared, too," she whispered, her uncanny insight taking away his breath again. He could almost believe she knew exactly why he was afraid.

He might be dragging them both straight to hell, but damned if he'd let her walk away again without kissing her.

Her lips curved in a smile as she read his expression with pinpoint accuracy. Before he'd dipped his head toward her, she was on her tiptoes, leaning into the kiss.

Oh, she felt good. Soft and warm, her kiss as sweet as Carolina honey. But beneath all the female temptation lay a core of Southern steel, tempered by the fiery heat of Alabama summers lived close to wild nature and polished to mirror shine by the tough Cooper blood that ran in her veins.

He'd never find anyone like her again. It didn't take a lifetime to understand that truth. He didn't have to know the minute details of her childhood to realize if he walked away from Shannon Cooper, his life would be poorer for it.

But what about her life? If he let her in, let her matter, would she regret it one day? Would that darkness inside him taint her, turn her generous affection into fear and hate?

She broke the kiss, laughing softly, oblivious to the maelstrom of emotions swirling wildly in his chest. "Gideon, what are we going to do?"

He knew what she was asking. "Nothing."

She continued laughing, although there was a hint of frustration in the display of mirth. "I think we're past that point."

He shouldn't touch her, should step back and let her walk away. But before he could get that thought through his aching head, his hand rose as if on its own volition to stroke her silky hair. "Let's get through the next couple of days. Get past the crisis and then we can decide what comes next."

She leaned her forehead against his chin. "I realize you probably couldn't have gleaned this from the past few days, but I'm not a particularly impulsive person."

He smiled. "Believe it or not, I did glean that." In some ways, she was remarkably cautious, taking care to arm herself when she confronted him on the boat, taking Lydia with her when they ran to fix the foghorn atop the lighthouse—even attacking him as he entered the caretaker's house had been a calculated risk rather than a reckless one. She'd known what she was doing and she'd damn near disarmed him.

"I was in love once." Her voice went very quiet, forcing him to lean closer to hear her. "It was fast and wild and a mistake of really painful proportions."

"We all have moments like that in our past," he said gently.

She looked up at him. "Not you. You don't take foolish risks. You're so controlled. It's like you think there's some dreadful beast inside you that you have to keep leashed at all times."

Once again, she floored him with her instinctive understanding of what really went on beneath the tough-hided, hell-for-leather marine he showed the world. He didn't know whether to be thrilled or terrified.

"Maybe there is." He dropped his hands away from her face.

"Is this about your father?"

He couldn't look at her. "He wasn't always a monster. I have good memories of him, too. But that just makes what he did all that more monstrous. And makes me wonder what I'm capable of—"

"You're his son, not his clone."

He shook his head. "I'm plenty like him." He thought about what she'd just said, how he acted as if there was a monster chained inside him, always in danger of breaking loose. That's exactly how he felt. "I've hurt people."

"You've killed a person in anger?" she asked, her gaze narrowed.

"No." He'd been angry enough to kill, but he'd never actually done it.

"You've hit someone in anger who didn't hit you first?"

"I've punched back harder than I needed to."

"Hard enough to cause permanent damage?"

"No," he admitted.

"I don't know what's happening here between us," she said quietly, her tone forcing him to look at her. Her dark eyes shined at him, full of anxiety but also bright with something else. Maybe hope. Or anticipation. "But I'm not afraid of you."

He wished he could feel anything but a bleak, creeping dread. Maybe, in time, she'd talk him into believing they had a chance to make things work. But time was something they had precious little of. Unless they got safely through the next forty-eight hours, none of it would matter anyway.

Chapter Fourteen

"You're going to let him kidnap me?" Lydia looked at the two of them as if they were insane. Shannon couldn't blame her.

"It's preemptive," Gideon explained, scooting his chair closer to Lydia's and taking her hand in his. "If they think Damon North has you, they're not going to send anyone else after you. You'll be safer with Damon than you would be anywhere else."

Lydia looked skeptical. "Even in police custody?"

"The police can't protect you a hundred percent," Shannon said firmly. She'd seen how easily police protection could be breached by people determined enough to take big risks. "There could be people right now on the local forces who are in the pockets of the bad guys."

"Terrebonne had a law enforcement scandal just last year," Gideon pointed out. "Shannon's cousins nearly lost their lives because of it."

Shannon glanced at Gideon, surprised. She'd never told him about the mess that had occurred the summer before, when her cousin's son had been kidnapped by a dangerous South American drug lord determined to use him to get revenge against Shannon's cousin Luke. Had he asked around?

Of course he would have, she realized. She'd mentioned her oblique connection to Natalie Becker through her cousin J.D. A couple of questions about Natalie Becker's new husband could have easily revealed the whole story of the Coopers' battle with Eladio Cordero's cartel in the piney woods outside Terrebonne.

That's our trouble, she thought. *Fascinated by each other, but too afraid to ask the interesting questions aloud.*

They'd come so close that morning outside her bedroom, cocooned in each other's heat. She'd almost told him that she was falling for him, hard. That she wanted it as much as she feared it.

She was terrified that she'd never get the chance to conquer her fears and follow the instincts that told her, whether ten days or ten years later, she'd still want to be wherever Gideon Stone was.

"Can I be armed?" Lydia asked, making both Shannon and Gideon laugh. Lydia smiled as well, but the look in her eyes was serious. "Edward bought me a Beretta last summer. We trained until I passed the test easily. I'd feel safer with it on me."

"I don't see why not," Shannon answered, looking at Gideon.

"I think we'll insist on it," Gideon agreed.

"You have a holster and ammunition?" Shannon asked.

"I do," Lydia answered. "So how will this happen?"

"I'll take Shannon into town as if she's leaving. Damon will come get you here at the house and call his associates, telling them he has you."

"Then what?" Lydia asked.

"Then we wait for someone to contact Gideon to make a deal."

One of Lydia's eyebrows lifted in a skeptical arch. "And then what?"

Gideon smiled, but Shannon could see tension in the fine creases around his eyes. "Then I stall until we can lure them into our trap."

Shannon couldn't blame Lydia for her unease. She wasn't

sure how she and Gideon were supposed to lure the other three operatives into a trap on the island. They had no assurance beyond Damon's promise that there weren't a bunch of other operatives waiting in the wings to ride to the rescue.

"We should get my family involved," she told him later when Lydia had gone out to her garden. "Safety in numbers."

She and Gideon sat on the front porch in the matching rockers, watching the storm clouds slowly rolling in from the Gulf.

"I don't think we can do that without drawing a lot of attention," Gideon said doubtfully.

"My cousins are all boaters. They can be down here in five hours with their boats."

"Look at those waves." He gestured toward the Gulf. "The *Lorelei* can handle it, but those bass boats your cousins drive won't be able to handle surf this rough."

Now she *knew* he'd asked questions about her and her family. "Then we smuggle them aboard the *Lorelei* and bring them here at night."

"I've already talked to your brother," Gideon said, turning to look at her. "I told him what we have planned."

She shook her head. "When?"

"Earlier this morning while you were taking a shower."

"You wanted him to talk me into going home."

"I wanted him to order you to go home."

She didn't know whether to laugh at the idea or smack him upside the head for even suggesting it. "Stop trying to handle me."

"I want you safe."

"I want to be safe, but because you seem to be intent on handling this without outside help, I'm all you've got for backup."

"So you're saying if I found someone else to back me up, you'd go home?" He looked at her, his eyebrows arched.

"No, I'm saying stop trying to treat me as if I'm breakable."

"You are," he said grimly. "Everyone is breakable."

She reached across the space between their chairs and touched his hand. He stared at her hand for a long moment, as if trying to figure out what to do. Finally, he turned his hand over, palm up, and threaded his fingers through hers, holding on tightly.

"What did Jesse say?" she asked.

"That you wouldn't come home if ordered, and he didn't run his agency the way he'd have run a unit in the Marine Corps." Gideon grimaced. "Sorry excuse for a Devil Dog."

Shannon smiled at the grim quip. "He has to trust the instincts of the people who work for Cooper Security or he'd never get anything accomplished. He sent me here because he knew I'd uncover the mystery if one really existed."

"He said he's been second-guessing that decision."

"I'm sure he has," Shannon said, trying not to take offense. The very fact that Jesse sent her at all was a huge step forward. "But he wasn't wrong. I found the journal. I recognized it as multilayered code."

"But what if we can't decode the journal without input from both Harlowe and Marsh?" Gideon shook his head. "We don't even know that we can decode it at all, now that General Ross is dead."

"The generals had to know it was possible one of them would die before the truth came out. Surely they had safeguards."

"Maybe they did," Gideon said, "but the one guy still alive who knows for sure isn't talking."

Shannon frowned. "What do you mean?"

"Your brother tried contacting General Marsh. He refused to take Jesse's call."

"Jesse's not his favorite person. Maybe someone else should try to reach him."

"Someone else did." Gideon gave her hand a light squeeze. She looked at him and found him gazing out toward the churning Gulf, his profile stony. "I called this morning. He wouldn't take my call, either."

"But if he doesn't know you—"

"He does. I worked under his command for over a year in Kaziristan. And I even met him again earlier this year, at General Ross's funeral." Gideon's gaze met hers. "We have to assume he realizes his fellow generals have met bad ends because of what they knew. In the case of General Marlowe, his family as well. General Marsh has his own hostages to think about."

His daughters, Shannon thought. His wife.

"Your brother says one of Marsh's daughters works for your company."

She nodded. "Evie, General Marsh's younger daughter. I guess she's in danger now, isn't she?"

"We have to assume so."

"I wonder if anyone's warned her."

"If not her father, I'm sure your brother has. He knows the danger."

She shook her head, feeling as if the world had turned entirely upside down in the past three days. "They're so bold—the SSU or whatever they call themselves now. They started an actual company, for heaven's sake."

"And maybe that'll help us bring them down. As far as your brother can tell, AfterAssets has never shown up in any investigations before. Now we've got the ball rolling."

"They'll just dump the company and start something new with some other SSU agent who hasn't yet shown up on anyone's radar."

"Maybe. But like cockroaches, they'll be a lot easier to stamp out scurrying around in the light than holed up somewhere in the dark." Gideon looked at his watch. "We need to leave in thirty minutes."

She nodded, pushing up from the rocker.

Inside, Lydia had returned from the garden and sat at the

kitchen table, weeping softly. Shannon hurried to her side, taking the older woman's hands between her own. "What's wrong?"

"I don't know why I bothered staking up the vegetables against the storm," she said, sniffing back her tears. "When I leave today, I may not ever be back."

"Of course you will."

Lydia shook her head. "I'll have to go somewhere safe, where I can't be found. You know that's what will have to happen, especially if you can't find a way to decode Edward's journal."

Shannon didn't try to argue against her point. Lydia's life wasn't going to be the same, no matter what happened over the next few days. Her husband was dead. She'd already agreed to sell the island to the state. Maybe grieving a little for the life she was leaving in the past was the best thing for her right now.

"Gideon and I are leaving in about thirty minutes. Damon's at the lighthouse if you need him before go-time—just hit the horn." She squeezed Lydia's hands. "Are you going to be okay?"

"I'll be fine."

Shannon headed upstairs to get ready for the trip to Terrebonne, wondering if any of them was ever going to be okay again.

GIDEON WAS GOING to miss piloting the *Lorelei.* He'd run a boat in his earlier days as a teenager growing up on the South Carolina coast, a fishing boat his uncle had owned before the economy turned sour and he'd lost the vessel to the bank. Uncle Phil had taken him in after the murder, the only family member willing to take in the angry, hostile teenager Gideon had been at the time.

After so many years away from the sea when he'd come to recuperate on Nightshade Island, he'd been a rusty sailor, but General Ross had been a patient teacher, using trips on the *Lorelei* as an incentive for Gideon to work hard to overcome the weakening effects of his shrapnel injuries and get back on his feet.

"You look at home behind the wheel."

He looked at Shannon, who sat next to him in the pilothouse. She was looking at him with curious brown eyes. "I used to pilot my uncle's fishing boat when I was a teenager. Some of my favorite memories."

"Where was that?"

"Fort Fremont in South Carolina. North of Hilton Head."

She smiled. "Went to Hilton Head with some girlfriends when I was nineteen. My dad worried the whole time I was away—first big trip without chaperones."

"Did you get in trouble?"

"*I* didn't," she said with a grin. "I didn't want to have to call home for help and risk the lecture. Mostly I just bummed around the beach, played a little volleyball, flirted with hot marines on leave from Parris Island." She slanted a look at him. "Who knows, maybe we met years ago."

He smiled. "I was probably already in Afghanistan by then. I'm a bit older than you."

"Not so much older," she murmured.

Heat swirled instantly between them, fueled by Shannon's smoldering gaze and his own vivid imagination, placing her on Coligny Beach in a little green bikini, showing off miles and miles of long, toned legs.

"What will you do when this is over?" she asked, her tone serious, although her eyes continued to suggest all sorts of delicious possibilities.

"When it's time to leave the island?"

She nodded.

He hadn't planned for anything in particular. Maybe he'd been as unwilling to think about the end of his life on the island as Lydia had been. The reality of time passing weighed heavily on him suddenly, a ball of lead sitting in the center of his chest.

"I guess I could go back to South Carolina," he said, thinking about the life he'd left behind there. His uncle was dead now, the last of his close family. He had some cousins on both sides of the family, but he knew few of them and had never been close to any. His uncle had died a bachelor, childless and penniless. "I suppose there's work to be had on the shrimp boats or fishing boats. Or maybe I'll look into age limits for joining the local police force."

"Is that something you'd like to do? Police work, I mean."

He thought about it. The investigative work would be interesting. He wasn't sure about the long hours of tedious patrol that would be required of him before he ever reached the level of investigator. Not to mention, it was entirely possible that, at thirty-four, he would be considered too old to be a prospect for any local cop shop.

"I don't know if I have the patience to be a rookie," he admitted.

"There's always security work."

He glanced at her. She was still looking at him with those sweet, sizzling brown eyes. He wanted her so much at that moment that he wasn't sure they'd ever make it to shore. Only the thought of Lydia's safety and their own important mission kept him from grabbing her hand and taking her down to the cabin this very minute.

What had she just said? Something about security work.

It took a second to follow the path her question laid out for him. "Security work as in, working for a security company?"

She blushed a little. "We're a growing company. Jesse started small and conservative so that he'd have means—and room—to expand. We've added several new agents recently and we're looking to hire more."

"But do you really need an old leatherneck? I mean, we must be a dime a dozen." The thought of going home with her when this was all done was too tempting to contemplate. He'd learned a long time ago that something that sounded too good to be true almost always turned out to be a disaster.

He'd been giving a lot of thought to the things they'd talked about the night before. He'd been worrying so long about the monster inside him that he'd lost sight of how many years he'd gone keeping it in check. Maybe that was the real difference between him and his father. His father had let stress and anger and a bone-deep meanness turn him into a killer. Gideon had honed his self-control and self-discipline until he could channel anger into constructive rather than destructive actions.

But even if he never turned out to be the beast he'd feared so many years, he wasn't much of a good bet for a relationship, either. What did he have to offer Shannon? He didn't even know what he wanted to do with his life. Maybe they should enjoy what was left of the time they had together for what it was and not try to shape it into something that would ultimately end in hurt feelings and broken hearts.

Hell, they didn't even know if they were going to survive the next couple of days, did they?

"I'll think about it," he said carefully, looking away.

When he dared another quick glance at her, she was no longer looking in his direction. Her delicate profile was pointing toward the mainland, where the shoreline grew closer and closer as the Hatteras cut through the choppy waters of the Gulf of Mexico.

The plan required them to go to lunch at Margo's Diner, where the talk would be about Shannon leaving town, her work complete. As expected, Margo wasn't shy about expressing her sorrow to see Shannon go. She passed along congratulations to Shannon's cousin J.D. and his new wife, Natalie, from about half the town as well, although Gideon suspected many of those well-wishers had merely responded to Margo's passing along of news with a simple "How nice."

"I can't believe that in a few weeks, there will no longer be a Stafford on Nightshade Island after all these years." Margo shook her head.

"Me, either," Gideon murmured, his heart sinking a little.

"Lydia's not going to be that far away from where I live," Shannon said with a smile. "Less than thirty minutes. I hope we'll stay in touch."

Gideon felt Shannon's gaze but didn't let himself return it. If she wanted to make the idea of working for her brother's company more tempting, she was doing a fine job. He had begun to think of Lydia Ross as family, virtually the only family he had anymore. He liked Lydia. Liked listening to her stories and her jokes. Liked their comfortable silences, their moments of quiet communion.

He liked that she somehow managed to look at him as if she were really seeing him for who he was rather than the man whose continued life had come at the price of her son's.

"I hope that doesn't mean we're losing you, too, handsome," Margo said with a flirtatious smile.

"I haven't decided yet," he admitted. "Not sure what jobs there are around here for an old Carolina beach bum like me."

Shannon cleared her throat.

"You're about as far from a beach bum as they get around these parts, marine," Margo said with a laugh.

He managed a grin. "Maybe so, but I don't have a platoon to lead around here, Margo. And I hear the Coopers ran the last of the terrorists out of town last year."

Unfortunately, a new set of vermin had taken their place. It might well be up to him and Shannon to run them out this time.

"I'll be right back," Shannon said, heading for the restrooms at the back of the restaurant. Gideon told himself not to watch her go, but he couldn't seem to drag his eyes from her curvy backside as she walked away on those long legs of hers, a relentless, impossible temptation.

Shannon disappeared into the restroom, and Gideon looked away with a sigh of frustration.

"You need to talk that girl into gettin' her brother to hire you, marine," Margo said softly.

"Her brother might have something to say about that."

"Like 'hell, yeah'?"

He smiled at her irrepressible matchmaking streak. "I'm not sure the Coopers will find me quite as irresistible as you do, gorgeous."

Margo beamed with pleasure at the compliment. "Maybe they'll like how sweet you are to that girl. Or how much you obviously think of her." She bent a little closer. "And I'm bettin' a big, strappin' fellow like you is pretty good to have around in a fight."

Gideon hoped she was right. He'd spent a lot of years training to be damn good in a fight. And he and Shannon might be on the verge of finding out just how good he really was.

Five minutes clicked past on the clock, and Shannon didn't come back from the restroom. Gideon's low-level unease began to blossom into full-blown anxiety. He looked at Margo, who had just come back from taking an order and was writing it up for the chef. "Shouldn't she be back by now?"

Margo looked surprised. "Want me to go check on her?"

"Would you?"

Margo pinned the order to the caddy by the kitchen door on her way to the bathrooms. The look on her face when she came back a few seconds later made Gideon's gut tighten to a hard knot.

"She's gone. The window in the bathroom's open." Margo held out her hand. "And I found this on the floor beneath the window."

Gideon looked down at her hand. On her palm lay Shannon's small silver watch, the stretch band snapped in half. And across the cracked crystal, there was a dark red smear of blood.

Chapter Fifteen

Her head hurt like hell, but at least she was still alive. She couldn't tell exactly where she was, unfortunately, other than somewhere inside a cramped, dark and stiflingly hot space.

Quelling a sudden rush of panic, Shannon wriggled until she could get her hands on something solid beneath her body. The rough, nubby texture of carpet rasped against her fingertips, and beneath that, the hard outline of a spare tire well. She was in a car trunk.

The panic clawed its way back.

The car didn't seem to be moving. She wasn't sure if that was good or bad. She couldn't remember much about what had happened between walking into the women's bathroom at Margo's and waking up in the trunk. She had no idea how much time had passed. The only thing she knew for sure, deep in her trembling gut, was that whoever had taken her hostage had no intention of letting her go alive.

The ache in her head was easing, reassuring her that she probably didn't have a closed head injury. She couldn't even be sure she had been hit on the head—the pain seemed to be internal rather than external. Maybe she'd been chloroformed. Or injected with something. Either would explain her general groggy feeling at the moment.

She fought against the urge to close her eyes and go back to the dreamless darkness from which she'd just emerged.

Wherever she was, she was running out of time to get out safely. No time for slumber.

Focus. You've had the training. What would a Cooper Security operative do in this situation?

First, figure out how she was bound.

Both hands and ankles were secured together by something hard and biting. Her hands were behind her back, the stress on her shoulders making them ache. By bending her wrists inward, she managed to touch her bindings with a couple of fingers. Hard plastic with ridges—flex cuffs. Better than metal cuffs at least, but still a bear to get out of.

She'd do better if she could get her hands around to the front, although thinking about the contortion required to do so made her head swim. She took a deep breath, trying to relax as much as possible, and tucked her knees up as close to her chest as she could in the cramped space. Her joints protested, making her wonder just how long she'd been lying immobile and contorted in this car trunk. Had more time passed than she believed?

Her shoulders felt stretched to the limit, but she managed to swing her arms forward, under her tucked up legs, until they were in front of her body instead of behind. She went limp for a few seconds afterward, letting her aching joints relax.

The pain subsided and she felt instantly more in control.

Had they thought to search her? Her GLOCK was gone—that was a given. But would they have thought to pat her down for other weapons?

She kept a small folding utility knife with her at all times. That wasn't a Cooper Security thing—her father had given all his kids utility knives as safety tools. Her particular version had a couple of flat blades, a saw blade and bottle and can opener blades. The saw should work on the flex cuffs, if her captors hadn't thought to look for weapons beyond her pistol.

She didn't keep the knife in a pocket, fortunately. She usually kept it tucked in her bra, snug against her skin where it wouldn't be seen. That particular trick *was* a Cooper Security thing—her sister Megan had taught her the wisdom of that hiding place. "You ever get grabbed by bad guys, the bra's the last place they'll think to look, unless they're looking to rape you. Then you got more problems than where you hide your knife."

She found the lump of the knife still there in her bra, tucked below her right breast. She released a soft breath of relief.

But before she could do anything, she heard the scrape of metal on metal, surprisingly loud in the darkness. A moment later, gray light flooded the area where she lay, blocked by a dark silhouette.

She blinked, her eyelids straining, against her will, to shut out the light.

She fought to keep them open, willed her eyes to adjust to the light more quickly. The dark silhouette remained where it was, looking down at her, until she started to make out more details.

Male. Dressed in all black, a knit balaclava covering the lower half of his face. A narrow oval of skin and eyes showed above the knit mask, revealing hooded hazel eyes and thick, sandy-brown eyebrows. She didn't recognize him, but there was little chance he was anyone other than one of the men Damon was working with.

"Look at you. You been busy," the man said with a flat Midwestern twang. "Got yourself all untwisted."

"My shoulders were aching," she retorted.

"No matter. You're not going anywhere anyway."

She didn't struggle when he reached into the car trunk and roughly grabbed the flex cuffs, using them to pull her up to a sitting position.

A second man came around the car and stood behind Midwest. Dressed in identical clothing, the only identifying features she could make out beneath the black mask were broad, high cheekbones, narrow eyes and the bridge of a straight nose. His skin color was ruddier than Midwest's, with a scattering of freckles across that straight nose. He didn't speak.

"Help me get her out," Midwest ordered.

She tried to remember what Margo had told her about the four men from the Azimut yacht. Damon, she knew already. And she'd described the man named Leo as a handsome charmer with blue eyes. Neither of these men fit that description. Damon had told them the fifth man, the yacht's pilot, was African-American as well.

So these two must be Raymond and Craig. Raymond was little, Margo had said. Craig was big and tall. The silent guy was definitely big and tall, and she supposed that under the ski cap, Raymond's hair might need a cut.

So, Raymond and Craig. Raymond was the one Gideon believed held a grudge against him. She'd have to remember that—not let him think there was any particular connection between the two of them. No need to invite more difficulties when she was in a bad place already.

"What do you want with me?" she asked.

Craig grabbed her around her hips, hauling her out of the trunk and down to the ground. He held on to her, enclosing both her wrists in the palm of his big hand. He must be the muscle, Shannon thought, wincing at the sheer strength of his grip.

It was raining now, a slow drizzle that created a false twilight of drab gray. They were in the middle of nowhere, surrounded on most sides by thick, piney woods, dotted in places with big, old hardwoods draped by silvery Spanish moss. The ground was soft beneath her feet, the air around her smelling of swamp. The car that had been her prison was an older model four-door Buick Regal. Black, with dark red interior. She memorized that image as well.

"Into the shack." Raymond nodded toward a small one-story cabin constructed of weathered gray pine. It looked rickety and old, and she had grave doubts about the rusty tin roof's ability to keep out the rain.

"We're not waiting for L—" Craig began to ask.

"Shut up!" Raymond snapped. "Just keep your mouth shut."

Craig's grip on Shannon's wrists tightened painfully, and she felt the tremble of barely chained violence in his hand.

"Where are we?" she asked aloud.

Raymond just gave her a withering look. "Don't worry about that, brown eyes. Shut up and do what we tell you. No questions."

She did as he said, knowing confrontation, however satisfying she might find it personally, would get her nowhere. The less she appeared to be a threat to them, the more they'd drop their guard, giving her a better chance to escape.

She did have one more question she decided to ask, however, thinking this might possibly be an answer they'd be willing to give. She waited until Craig settled her inside the shack and hooked her ankle cuffs to a chain set into the wall. She almost smiled at the criminal lack of forethought in that act. They apparently did see her as an easy mark.

It made her wonder how much they knew about her identity. She assumed they knew her name, probably even where she worked. Cooper Security might have given them pause—until they found out she was a computer geek who worked in IT, not as a field operative.

Please underestimate me, she pleaded silently.

As Craig stepped back and looked down at her, his narrow-eyed expression hard to read, especially with half his face hidden behind the balaclava, she asked, "What are you going to do with me?"

It was Raymond who answered. "You're leverage, sweetheart."

About what she expected. But she might as well play it with feigned ignorance. "Leverage for what?"

"You don't know?" he mocked.

"I don't," she said as innocently as she could. "I'm supposed to be on my way home right now. If I don't get there, my family's going to come looking for me, you know."

"Not soon enough."

Her stomach tightened into a knot at the hard promise she heard in his words. "We don't have money. It's all tied up in the company, untouchable. I don't know what you think ransom will accomplish."

"We don't want money," Raymond said, a mean smile dancing in his hazel eyes.

They want the journal, she thought. But aloud, she asked, "Then what?"

"That's not your concern." He nodded for Craig to follow him. "Let's go. We've got things to do before you-know-who gets back."

As they went through the open door, she called out, "Are you just leaving me here? Where are you going?"

Neither Raymond nor Craig turned around. The door shut behind them and she heard the rattle of a lock engaging.

She sat quietly for a couple of minutes, until she heard the sound of the car engine firing up outside. It purred a minute, then was gone, fading into the distance.

She pulled up the hem of her shirt and slid her fingers under the bra band, retrieving the knife. Listening anxiously for any sound outside the shack that might suggest her captors were returning, she fumbled with the knife, nearly dropping it twice, before she managed to flip open a small but sharp saw blade. She went to work on the cuffs, scraping her wrists a few times when the blade slipped but snapping them open in just a few minutes.

She rubbed her bleeding wrists for a second to soothe the pain, then went to work on the flex cuffs binding her ankles, freeing herself from the chain that held her in place.

Outside, rain was falling harder, but running through a

downpour sounded a lot better than holing up inside that shack, worrying about who'd show up next.

She didn't try the locked door, opting for one of the windows. With a little effort, she climbed out and landed lightly on the ground outside the cabin.

All she had to do was make her way out of these woods and back to some place with a phone.

It was a simple plan. Simple plans were always the best.

But only when they worked.

THE BATHROOM WINDOW at Margo's Diner opened to a small back alley used primarily for deliveries and garbage removal. A narrow margin of summer-dried grass lay just beneath the window, giving way to gravel within a couple of feet.

The falling drizzle hadn't yet penetrated the sun-hardened soil enough to create a muddy surface for footprints. Gideon stared in painful impotence at the open window and tried to picture what had happened.

Someone had ambushed her in the bathroom. Subdued her somehow—force, perhaps, or even something like a knockout drug. Just enough to get her outside without a fight.

How had they known she was in the bathroom?

"Gideon?" Margo's hesitant voice, just a few feet away, snapped his attention her way. He saw she was standing next to a skinny teenaged girl with lanky dark blond hair and tear-reddened blue eyes.

"What?" he asked, trying not to let his fear and anger show.

"Go on, Deenie, tell him," Margo urged the weeping blonde. "He won't bite, I promise."

Gideon struggled to keep his expression calm. "What is it?"

"This is Deenie Albertson. Tell him what you told me."

Haltingly, Deenie spoke, her voice hitching with quiet sobs. "I swear, he said it was just a joke! And I needed the money to help pay my way to the choir competition this winter, and I didn't see any harm—"

"Who said it was a joke?" Gideon curled his fingers into fists.

"He said his name was Ray, and he was so funny about it—told me his girlfriend had been waitin' and waitin' for him to pop the question, and he wanted to make it memorable. He was going to jump through the window into the ladies' bathroom, see, while she was in there and propose right then and there—'cause it would be real memorable, see?" Deenie wiped her eyes.

"How was he supposed to get in there?"

"I went and unlocked the bathroom window. I was supposed to get her in there somehow if she didn't go alone, but then she just went by herself and I had to hurry outside and tell him she was in there."

"I didn't see him in the diner," Margo murmured.

"He didn't go inside," Deenie said. "He caught me outside, pointed her out through the window and then gave me twenty bucks to do it. But I didn't know it was a lie!"

He said his name was Ray.

Gideon bit back a profanity and turned away, his stomach in a knot. If Raymond Stephens had Shannon, and had any idea of the connection between them, she was in serious danger. Ray's grudge-holding had been legendary in the marine unit where he'd spent his aborted military career.

How far would he go, what measures would he take, to make sure Gideon suffered for the unforgiveable sin of thwarting Raymond Stephens?

"Did you see what he was driving?" he asked Deenie.

She shook her head.

The faint trill of a phone filtered past his worry, drawing his attention to the ground nearby. He hurried over and found a small black phone—the exact make Shannon used.

He picked it up, saw the name on the display. Jesse Cooper.

He hit the answer button. "Cooper?"

There was a brief pause on the other end of the line, filled with the loud roar of some sort of engine. Jesse's voice finally came, raised to override the background noise. "Stone?"

"Yeah," he answered, dreading what he had to say next.

"Where's my sister?" Already, Gideon heard a tone of accusation in the other man's voice.

He felt an answering flood of guilt wash through him as he spoke the words he never wanted to say.

"She's been taken."

OVERHEAD, THE SKY was only partly cloudy, the rain easing off for the moment. A watery sun came out, turning the woods into a sauna, but the heat was enough to start drying Shannon's clothes to a bearable dampness.

Unfortunately, as she headed south in search of civilization, the soft, loamy ground beneath her feet gave way to marshland, soaking her sneakers and bottom half of her jeans. Mosquitoes and flies buzzed through the air around her, a constant nuisance, but she couldn't take time or attention to bat them away, for with marshlands came far more immediate dangers, like water moccasins and alligators.

All roads south led to the shoreline. If she could get to the shore, she could find civilization, for there were few pieces of the Gulf Coast shoreline left undeveloped. But apparently the only way to get to the Gulf was to wade through the increasingly swampy wetlands she was slogging through. If she didn't watch her step—

A soft hiss was all the warning she got.

She hit reverse immediately, barely avoiding disaster as a small mossy-backed alligator rose up from a nearby bog, snapping at her with an explosive crash of massive jaws and deadly sharp teeth.

She scrambled backward, splashing across sodden ground. One of her shoes stuck in the muck, threatening to pin her in place, but she jerked it free and scuttled farther back, onto firmer ground, her pulse so thunderous in her ears she could barely hear the ragged rasp of her breath.

The alligator didn't seem inclined to follow her out of the water, so she backtracked a little farther, deciding to keep to more solid ground on her trek south.

With the rain having abated for now, she could guide herself by the position of the sun. It was already dipping westward to her right, so as long as she could keep the sun generally on that side of her, she'd be headed south, even if she had to detour now and then to avoid the water.

Gideon had to be wondering where she was by now. Had someone seen her being abducted? Her wrist still ached where her captors had ripped her watch off in the struggle—had they realized it had come off? Had they picked it up and brought it with them?

She also didn't have her phone, but Ray and Craig may have taken that off her when they took her GLOCK.

Gideon had to be looking for her by now. He'd know she wouldn't just hare off on him, wouldn't he?

The sound of whistling slowly entered her consciousness, and a flood of relief washed over her at the first sound of human civilization she'd come across in what felt like hours. But she couldn't afford to be foolish. For all she knew, one of her captors had doubled back, found her missing, and followed her into the swamp.

She crouched behind a wide bladed palmetto bush and watched cautiously as the whistler hiked into view.

It was a man in his early thirties. Hard to say if he was handsome or not, with his head down and covered with a camouflage baseball cap. He wore a dark T-shirt and faded jeans, with a lightweight olive green slicker-style jacket that still glistened with rain drops from the most recent shower. He carried a long pole with a three-pronged steel gig at the end of it, and a large olive-green rucksack. He continued whistling as he strode unhurriedly past her, deeper into the swamp.

It was a little early in the evening for frog gigging, but maybe he knew a place that took a while to reach. Or maybe he just couldn't stay out here late at night and preferred, while surrounded by cranky alligators, to be able to see where he was putting his foot as he walked.

Just stand up. Call out. Ask for help.

He looked friendly enough, the pleasant tune he whistled as he strolled through the swamp reminiscent of a song her father had taught her to whistle years ago, when she was just a little girl.

Of course, there were other things her father had taught her when she was a little girl.

Never talk to strangers.

But sometimes a stranger could save your life.

Taking a deep breath, she stood up and called out. "Hello!"

The frog gigger jumped at the sound of her voice, whirling around. He looked alarmed, pressing his hand against his chest.

"You scared the life out of me, ma'am! Are you lost?" He spoke in a thick, nasal country accent, slow and drawling. But his eyes looked friendly and the smile he shot her way made her feel more at ease.

"I'm lost," she said, deciding to keep it simple. "I need to get back to Terrebonne. Can you help me?"

"Sure." He walked back to where she stood. "What did you do, wander off from a hiking party or something?"

"Something like that," she said, not willing to freak out her friendly rescuer with the truth. "If you can just get me to civilization, I can take it from there. Or—do you have a cell phone? I could just call someone to come here to get me."

"Sure, I've got a phone." He looped the handles of the rucksack over one finger of the hand holding the frog gig and pulled his phone from his pocket with his free hand. He held it out to her.

She reached for the phone, nearly wilting with relief.

Until he whipped the frog gig forward and pressed it against her throat.

She froze, not even wincing as the sharp tip of the gig pricked the flesh at the base of her throat. The man smiled at her slowly, the skin crinkling around his startling blue eyes.

He put the phone in his pocket and caught her arm. "You're a whole lot of trouble, you know?" The drawl was gone, replaced by a cultured Northeastern accent she placed somewhere in upper New England.

She lifted her chin, fighting the flood of despair rattling her knees. "And you, I presume, must be Leo."

Chapter Sixteen

"I'm less than an hour from Terrebonne," Jesse told Gideon over the engine roar, which he explained was the sound of a helicopter rotor. He said his cousin J.D., a former navy chopper pilot, was behind the controls, and he'd brought other reinforcements.

"I thought you said you didn't want to get involved yet."

"Changed my mind. What are you doing to find Shannon?"

Gideon didn't want to admit there wasn't much he could do. She'd simply vanished from the diner. "I'm trying to find a witness, see if anyone spotted a strange vehicle around—"

"What about prints, evidence—"

"We both know who has her." Just not what they'd do with her.

Jesse fell silent.

"Do you have a place to land?" Gideon asked.

"J.D.'s friend has a hangar at the local airport. He can set down there and we can meet you."

"I'm going to be looking for witnesses—maybe we can figure out what sort of vehicle her kidnappers were driving."

"Stay in touch." It was a warning, not polite small talk.

J.D. hung up Shannon's phone and tucked it in the pocket of his jeans. Holding on to it for her, just as he was holding on to the broken watch. Small totems reminding him how essential she'd become to him in such a short amount of time.

She had to be alive. If they wanted her dead, he'd have found her in the bathroom in a pool of her own blood. They needed her alive for some reason, and all she had to do was keep her head down until Gideon could find her.

But would she do that? Would she just sit there and be a complacent hostage, waiting for her rescuer?

Hell, no. That wasn't the Shannon Cooper he knew. She'd push back. She'd try to escape. And she might well get herself killed.

"Gideon?"

He looked up at the sound of Margo's voice. She stood nearby, next to a tall, lean man in his early thirties, dressed in a lightweight suit. *Cop,* Gideon thought.

"This is Doyle Massey, with the Chickasaw County Sheriff's Department."

Gideon supposed it was inevitable that someone would call the law. He nodded at Massey. "Gideon Stone."

Massey walked over slowly, his gaze on Gideon's face as if assessing the mood. "You want to catch me up on things?"

It was the last thing Gideon wanted to do. "Who called you?"

"Does it matter?"

He supposed not. "My friend went to the bathroom. She didn't return, and when Margo went to check on her, we found the window open and this lying on the floor." He showed Massey the broken watch, now safely encased in a plastic zip-top bag.

"Blood?" Massey asked, nodding at the red spot on the watch crystal.

"I think so. Probably scraped her wrist when it tore off."

"What's your friend's name?"

"Shannon Cooper."

Massey's eyes narrowed. "Kin to J. D. Cooper?" Massey asked.

"Cousin."

Massey sighed. "This isn't connected to a South American drug cartel by any chance?"

Gideon shook his head. "No." *Just a group of ruthless, deadly mercenaries.*

As Massey was about to ask another question, Gideon's cell phone rang. Checking the display, he saw a number he didn't recognize and almost ignored the call. Then he realized whoever had Shannon might contact him with demands.

Excusing himself, he took the call. "Stone."

The male voice on the other end of the line was smooth and articulate, the accent Northern and educated. His pleasant tone clashed with his words. "Mr. Stone, you have something I want. And I have something you want."

Gideon felt his muscles contract with rage, but he tried to remain outwardly calm, well aware that Deputy Massey was a few feet away, watching him with deep curiosity. "Who is this?"

"Someone not stupid enough to share that information with you."

"It's Leo." That was Shannon's voice, strong and angry, close to the receiver. "We're in a swamp—"

A soft gasp cut off her words, and Leo's voice came over the line again, a little strained. "Now you know what I have. Want to trade?"

"If you hurt her—"

"Yeah, I know, you'll hunt me down and kill me like a rabid dog." Leo sounded bored. "Let's not make this hard, okay? You don't know what's in the journal anyway. It's coded, and you're not going to find the keys to decode it. So, really, it's not a hard choice."

Gideon kept his voice low, acutely aware of Massey's presence nearby. "Are the Harlowes still alive?"

The question seemed to surprise Leo. He didn't answer immediately.

"That's how you know about the journal, right?" Gideon pressed.

"Aren't you a clever boy?" Leo asked quietly.

"Don't give it to him!" That was Shannon again.

"Shut up!" Leo snapped.

"Where do you want to meet?" Gideon asked.

"I'll call back." The line went dead.

"Was that your friend?" Massey asked, closer than Gideon expected.

He looked at the deputy, wondering how much he'd heard. "No."

"Let me rephrase," Massey said quietly. "Was that the person or persons who have your friend?"

"I don't know where she is."

"That's not what I asked."

Gideon took a step toward Massey, crowding him. He had a five-inch advantage on the other man, so he might as well put it to use. "Am I under arrest?"

Massey's eyes narrowed. "No."

"Then I'll be going." He walked over to where Margo stood, watching with worried eyes, and squeezed her arm. "I have to go."

"Did you find her?"

"Not yet," he said grimly.

But soon.

LEO STILL HADN'T produced a gun, Shannon realized as she walked slowly through the marsh in front of him and his sharp-pronged frog gig. It didn't mean he didn't have one on him, but for whatever reason, he'd decided to keep it hidden and rely on the gig pole to keep her under his control.

It was working well enough, she thought bleakly. She was still bleeding a little where he'd pricked her throat with the prongs. It would be just about her luck if that gator she'd passed earlier smelled the blood and came hunting.

Which wouldn't necessarily be a bad thing, she realized, scanning the swampy woods ahead of her for any sign of familiar territory. She'd run into the gator near a fallen oak tree, she remembered, mistaking the moss-backed reptile for tree root sticking out of the water until he'd snapped at her.

A fallen oak tree lay about thirty yards ahead, close to a watery bog. Was it the same tree? It appeared to be straight ahead, right in their path. If they passed it, was there a way to coax the gator to make another appearance?

Her shoes squished loudly in the mud as they walked. She hoped the alligator was listening.

"You're awfully quiet," Leo murmured behind her.

"Just trying to figure out what you really want." She kept her eye on the bog beside the fallen tree. There was a grayish-green mass barely visible above the waterline. Was that her friend the alligator?

"I told your boyfriend what we want."

"But why?"

"Can't tell you that."

The shape of the mass in the water looked about right. If she could just get Leo on that side of her when they passed—

"I've heard about the Coopers," Leo said. "Our nemeses, I guess you'd say," he added with a laugh. "Never heard anything about you, though."

"I'm just a computer geek," she said drily, edging closer to the bog.

"Why did they send you on this job, then?"

"It's archiving. I'm an archivist."

Now, she thought as they reached the edge of the water.

"Ow!" She stopped and bent, shifting to the side, away from the water.

As she'd hoped, Leo didn't stop when she did, his forward momentum taking him halfway around her, perilously close to the bog.

The gator surged from his watery hiding place, jaws snapping.

Leo cried out, scrambling back. He toppled to his backside, dropping the frog gig. He also dropped his cell phone as he fell. It bounced off Shannon's foot and landed right in front of her.

She scooped it up and started running.

A sharp report shattered the air behind her. She didn't know if Leo was shooting at the alligator or at her. She didn't stop to check. Splashing through the marsh, she zigzagged the best she could, seeking the cover of tree trunks as she wound her way north, deeper into the swamp.

The ground grew firmer soon, but she wasn't any closer to recognizable signs of civilization. She could still hear the sounds of movement in the swamp behind her, but Leo was far enough away for her to stop and get her bearings.

The sun was gone again, dipping behind a dark band of clouds overhead. Rain had resumed falling, deepening the shadows in the woods around her.

She had no idea where she was. For all she knew, she might be just yards away from the shack from which she'd escaped. Ray and Craig might be close by, waiting for Leo to bring her back to captivity.

She looked down at the cell phone still clutched in her tightened fist. Sending up a silent prayer for a signal, she flipped it open and looked at the display panel.

No bars.

She hung up, slid the ringer to vibrate, and put it in her bra with the folding knife. If it rang, she'd feel it, even if she couldn't hear it.

She listened carefully to the forest sounds, trying to discern between natural noises and any signs that Leo was headed her way. If he was moving toward her, she couldn't hear him at all.

Maybe he'd gone still, listening for her.

She felt a flutter of confidence beating slowly but steadily in her chest. Driving a boat wasn't the only thing she'd learned from her cousins as a child. Jake and Gabe, the best trackers in the family, had taken her under their wing and taught her all sorts of arcane things about moving silently through the woods. The swamp wasn't exactly Gossamer Mountain, territory as familiar to her as the freckles on her face. But the same basic rules applied. Move silently. Be deliberate. Leave no signs.

And sometimes, the best camouflage was being perfectly still.

THE LAST THING Gideon expected to see when he took the *Lorelei* back to Nightshade Island was a sleek gray Bell 206L LongRanger sitting on the flat edge of the beach near the boathouse. Four large, broad-shouldered and dark-haired men huddled together near the side of the bird. All four turned at the sound of the Hatteras motoring toward the boathouse, and Gideon saw what their huddled bodies had hidden from his view: Damon North stood next to the helicopter, straightening his clothes with sharp, irritated movements.

Gideon bypassed the boathouse and slid the Hatteras up next to the external pier, looping a rope over the pilings. So these were the Coopers.

"Stone?" The speaker was a broad-shouldered man in his mid-thirties, with coffee-brown eyes and a perpetual look of suspicion in his even features. He was about four inches shorter than Gideon, with a steel-spined posture that pegged him as a former marine. His air of authority suggested leadership.

"Jesse Cooper," Gideon guessed aloud. "I thought you were landing at the local airport."

"We decided not to advertise our arrival." The man who answered was a tall, rangy man in his early forties, dressed in camouflage pants and an olive drab T-shirt. He stood near the pilot's door of the Bell helicopter. He must be J.D., the cousin.

Jesse Cooper got to the point. "Any word on my sister?"

Gideon dreaded what he had to tell the man. "I got a call from the man who has her. I know him only as Leo."

A third man gave a small start. "Leo Reed?"

Gideon looked at him more closely. He was taller than Jesse Cooper, shorter than the pilot. Dark-haired, dark-eyed, well-built. He looked a little queasy.

This must be Rick Cooper, Gideon thought. The brother who'd worked for MacLear. "I don't know."

"It's Reed." Damon spoke up for the first time. "He's the leader."

The others looked at Damon, their expressions dark.

Gideon remembered the masked man he'd seen in the woods. The one who'd looked to be in charge. That must have been Reed. "What do you know about him?"

"He was regular MacLear," Rick said grimly. "I worked with him on a few cases. Seemed straight enough."

"Money is a temptress," said the fourth person, a quiet man in his mid-thirties. Another former marine, he guessed. Shannon's other brother?

As it turned out, it was a cousin. "Sam Cooper." He nodded toward the others in order. "Shannon's brothers Rick and Jesse and my brother J. D. Cooper."

"You're the one who married Natalie Becker," Gideon murmured, looking at J.D. "Nice wedding picture."

J.D. frowned, but Gideon didn't have time to explain. He waved toward the boat. "She's somewhere in a swamp. You can't take the bird to get to her. We'll go in the boat."

"Leo told you where he was?" Rick asked, sounding confused, as they started moving toward the boat.

Gideon put his hand out and pushed against Damon's chest as he started to follow. "Where is Lydia?"

Damon stared back at him, not answering.

Gideon tightened his grip on the front of the man's shirt, rage flooding through him like blood in his veins. "Where is she?"

"She's safe."

Gideon balled his free hand into a fist, struggling with the urge to smash the man's face until he bled. He controlled it, barely. "Where is she?"

"She's with Quinn, isn't she?" Rick's voice cut through Gideon's anger.

"Yes," Damon admitted.

"Who's Quinn?" Gideon demanded.

"CIA," Jesse answered. "He won't let anything happen to her."

"CIA?" Gideon looked from Jesse to his brother, not missing the look of wariness in Rick Cooper's eyes. "What's going on here?"

"We know about the journal. Shannon told us about it."

"What's in it?" Gideon asked.

"We're not sure," Jesse answered.

Gideon didn't have time to hash things out. Shannon was out there, somewhere, in the custody of a rogue mercenary willing to kill her to get what he wanted. The rest of the mystery—even the secret of what happened to Ford Ross—could wait until Gideon got her back.

"Watch him," Gideon told the others. "I'll be right back."

He ran up the path, detouring to the caretaker's house. Earlier that morning, before heading to the mainland, he and Shannon had locked the general's coded journal beneath a pile of Gideon's old Marine Corps memorabilia in Gideon's footlocker. Shannon had tucked the journal inside Gideon's ripped-up flak jacket, the one he'd torn off to make himself lighter for Ford Ross's rescue attempt. It had been shredded by the shrapnel from the exploded grenade. It still had Ford's blood on it, as well as his own.

She had looked up at him with solemn, haunted eyes. "So close."

He'd cupped her cheek, bending for a swift, fierce kiss. Her hands had curled in the fabric of his T-shirt, holding him close as she kissed him back.

He shouldn't have let her go.

He changed into camouflage gear, tucking the journal into the roomy pocket on the side of his trouser leg, and hurried back to the chopper.

"Get on the boat," he said to the others, turning to pin Damon North with a dark look. "Except you. You stay here and stay out of trouble."

"Don't do this, Gideon. Don't make a trade with the journal."

Gideon ignored him, striding quickly to the boat.

The pilot, J.D., shot a warning look toward North. "Touch my bird and I'll hide you and hang you up to dry. Got it?"

North grimaced but nodded. "Got it."

The rest of them boarded the boat. Almost immediately, Rick and Sam flanked either end of the boat, while J.D. stood on the deck, watching Damon North with suspicion as they shoved off.

Jesse climbed up to the pilothouse with Gideon. "Did you talk to Shannon when Leo contacted you?"

"No, but I heard her." He told Jesse what Shannon had said.

"Swamp could mean any marshy place, and there are dozens of those all along the coast." Jesse's tone was grim. "Where do we even start?"

Gideon didn't know. He just knew he had to find her. She had begun to give him hope for a future he'd never thought he could have. Bit by tiny bit, her kindness and her show of faith in him had started to convince him he wasn't doomed to become a monster like his father. He almost believed it now. Maybe he could be a good man, a loving man. A family man.

He'd already lost nearly everyone who'd ever mattered

to him in this life. If he lost Shannon, too, there wouldn't be anything left of him to save.

SHANNON HEARD A sound, out in the woods. Footsteps, moving with too much speed to remain quiet. She hunkered down in the little hiding place she'd found for herself, tucked between a fallen pine tree trunk and a scrubby stand of thick green shrubs she couldn't identify. The ground beneath her was spongy but mostly dry. Her situation could be worse, she supposed, although it was hard to keep her spirits up with a stranger splashing through the bog just twenty yards away.

She dared a peek and spotted the man she now knew as Raymond moving as quickly as he could through the marsh. She looked around him, seeking any sign of the other one, Craig, but Raymond seemed to be alone.

She sat in utter silence until he passed out of sight. The sounds of the mud sucking at his boots faded into silence again.

She had to get out of here. Even if the SSU agents didn't find her, she couldn't just hunker down and stay awhile. Gideon thought she was in Leo's custody. He'd be frantic with worry and guilt.

She pulled the phone from her bra and checked the signal. No bars.

She listened carefully for the slightest hint of human movement around her. There was nothing. The sounds of birds in the trees had returned, however, after going silent while Raymond splashed by.

She took a chance and moved from her hiding place.

No bullets whizzed through the air toward her. No burst of movement in the swamp around her as the hunter spotted his prey.

Overhead, the sun had broken through again, lower in the sky. That way was west, then. She decided to go north. North would take her away from the beach, but it would take her closer to inland towns that might boast a cell tower with a good signal.

She trekked about half a mile and stopped, pulling the phone out and checking the signal.

Her heart flip-flopped at the five shining bars on the signal indicator. A nice, strong connection, for the moment at least.

She didn't have any idea what Gideon's cell phone number was, she realized, but the last call on Leo's phone had been to Gideon. Holding her breath, she hit redial.

Gideon answered on the first ring, his voice steely with rage. Engine noise hummed in the background. "Yes?"

"It's me," she said, as softly as she could.

"Shannon?" Gideon's voice broke. She heard an exclamation somewhere on his end and recognized her brother's voice.

"Is Jesse there with you?"

"Yes. Where are you?"

"I got away but I'm lost, and Leo's somewhere out here. He has a gun and a frog gig—" She managed a wobbly grin. "I ran him into a gator and got away. He dropped his phone so I grabbed it."

His voice grew stronger. "Crazy, brave girl."

"I'm still in a swamp. I don't know where. Maybe close to town, maybe a long way away. I was out for a little while and I woke up in a car trunk, so I didn't get my bearings—"

"Are you hurt?"

"No." Minor aches and scrapes, but they weren't worth mentioning. "Raymond and Craig were the ones who grabbed me. They put me in a cabin somewhere in the swamp." She described what she could remember of the cabin. "I cut myself free as soon as they left, but Leo caught me out in the swamp. I'm sorry—he looked like someone who'd help me."

"You did amazing," Gideon said.

"I just saw Raymond Stephens a few minutes ago. I didn't see anyone else. He didn't see me."

"Good." Gideon sounded profoundly relieved. "Is there anywhere you can hide until I can come find you?"

She looked around, trying to see anything remotely familiar about her surroundings. "I think I might be close to the cabin," she decided. "I can't go back there, but if you could figure out where it is—"

"I know just who to ask," he said firmly. "Hang up the phone and put it on vibrate. I'll call you back as soon as I can—"

There was a small commotion on the other end of the line. The next thing she heard was her brother Jesse's voice. "Shan? It's me. Tell me you're okay. Are you hurt?"

"I'm fine. I'm just a little wet and a whole lot scared." She blinked back tears, refusing to let them fall. "What are you doing there?"

"Coming to get you, darlin'." Jesse's voice softened. "I'm so sorry for sending you down here without even telling you why."

"We'll talk about that when I see you again. But stop kicking yourself." She thought about all she'd been through over the past few days, the friendship she'd found in Lydia and the excitement and passion of her roller-coaster feelings for Gideon, and she couldn't regret a thing except letting herself be taken hostage in the first place. "I'm fine. Cooper Security taught me well. Just get here soon, okay?"

"Hunker down and stay out of sight. Can you do that?"

She grinned, feeling hope for the first time. "If there's anything a Cooper knows how to do, it's hide in the woods."

Chapter Seventeen

"Who's this person we're going to see?" Rick Cooper's voice was edged with frantic impatience as Gideon led them to the garage unit at the Terrebonne Marina.

"It's a man who knows the backwoods around here like his own reflection in the mirror," Gideon answered, keying open the padlock and opening the garage door. He'd have preferred to take the truck, but even the extended cab wouldn't accommodate all five of them. He unlocked the Cadillac instead and motioned them inside.

"Wouldn't happen to be Rudy Lawler, would it?" J.D. slid into the front passenger seat next to him, leaving the backseat to his brother and cousins.

"You know him?" Gideon asked.

"Met him once." A smile played with J.D.'s mouth, as if the memory amused him. "Sure you can get him to cooperate?"

"I have my ways," Gideon said grimly.

J.D. muttered something that sounded like "jarhead." Gideon let it pass, concentrating on backing out of the garage without hitting anyone in his haste to get to Rudy's place.

Even though his land butted up to some pretty expensive property just off County Road 9, Rudy Lawler lived in a small, cluttered bungalow that had seen better days. The clapboard siding was weathered and faded, once a lively yellow but now a dingy, mud-spattered dun. An old Buick sat in the side yard, tires missing, propped on cinderblocks. More rust than blue paint covered its dented chassis, and kudzu was growing up over the back window.

At the sound of the Cadillac, Rudy Lawler stepped out of the house, cradling a Remington 700 rifle. Gideon sighed, not in the mood to have to talk him down, but before he could make a move, J.D. got out of the car and walked toward Rudy, showing no sign of fear.

"Hey, Rudy, remember me?" J.D. called.

Eyes narrowing, Rudy tightened his grip on the Remington. "You're that big gorilla who tried to knock my head off out in the woods behind that restaurant, ain't you?"

Gideon looked at the others. "Stay put." He got out and joined J.D. in the yard. "Hey, Rudy."

"What do y'all want?" Rudy asked suspiciously.

"We're looking for a cabin. Somewhere secluded," J.D. said.

"Somewhere marshy, where you'd find alligators."

Rudy looked from one to the other of them, his brow furrowed. "You wantin' to hide out or something?"

"What if we did?" Gideon asked. "Where would you send us?"

Rudy seemed to give it a little thought. "Cypress Grove," he said finally. "About ten miles east of here, near the wildlife reserve."

"You know how to get there?"

"I can draw you a map," he answered. "Stay here. I'll be right back."

As Rudy disappeared inside, Gideon looked at J.D. "Big gorilla that tried to take his head off?"

"Long story."

Rudy came back, holding a grubby-looking sheet of paper. He handed it to Gideon. "Watch your step. There's gators in that swamp as big as either one of you."

Gideon's stomach tightened at the thought, his fear less for himself and more for Shannon, who might be a tough, brave woman but was no match for a pissed-off alligator.

"You drive, I'll navigate," he told J.D., handing him the keys to the Cadillac. He got in the passenger side and unfolded the crudely drawn map, trying to figure out what was what.

Rudy had supplied the roads into the swamp, calling them not by their official names but by the local monikers the roads had borne for decades. Gideon wasn't a Terrebonne native, but he'd made a point of living as the locals did once it was clear he was going to be here awhile, tasked with protecting the general and Lydia. He'd approached the job the way he'd approach special missions in battle zones—listen to the locals, get to know their customs and their ways, learn everything he could about every nuance of life in the area.

He knew that "Old Grove Road" was County Highway 14, a winding two-lane road that ran all the way from Terrebonne to the Mississippi state line. The small curvy turnoff Rudy had labeled "Sycamore Road" must be the dirt road that seemed to lead to nowhere just after you passed mile marker number twelve.

"Know where we're headed?"

Gideon nodded, pointing him toward Highway 14. "We're going to have to park somewhere eventually and go on foot. I'll let you know when we get there."

They were about two miles from the turnoff when J.D. made a low, murmuring sound deep in his throat.

"What is it?" Rick asked from the backseat.

"Don't turn around. Just keep looking forward." J.D.'s voice was low and tense. His gaze kept flicking toward the rearview mirror.

Gideon darted a glance at the side mirror. There was a black sedan behind them, about seventy yards back. "The sedan?" he asked.

"It's stuck with us the whole way so far. Same distance back, no matter how fast or slow I go."

"We're coming up on a traffic light," Gideon said. "He'll have to come closer if we get stopped there."

Ahead, the light at the intersection with Highway 6 went from yellow to red. As much as Gideon chafed at the idea of stopping instead of shooting through the yellow light, he held his tongue. He directed J.D. to adjust the side mirror controls as the sedan pulled closer to give him a better look at the driver. There was little glare on the windshield, thanks to the cloud cover, allowing Gideon a good look at the driver of the Buick sedan.

Big guy. Short, dark hair and a pugnacious jaw. At a guess, it might be the one named Craig. The muscle, he thought, rage burning in his gut. But instead of making him feel out of control, the anger acted as fuel, coursing like lifeblood through his veins. He channeled his fury, let it strengthen him and focus him.

"Do you recognize him?" Rick asked quietly.

"I think it might be a guy we know as Craig. J.D., adjust the mirror until Rick says stop." He waited for Rick Cooper's assessment.

"Craig Linden," Rick murmured. "Army washout, dishonorably discharged. He's one of the former SSU agents on the FBI watch list."

The light turned green. "We have about two miles to go to the turnoff," Gideon told J.D. "Around a mile out, there's a sharp curve that will hide us from the Buick. If he keeps back seventy yards or so, I'll have about five seconds to exit the car and hide."

J.D. shot him a disbelieving look. "And what, we just head on down the road like decoys?"

"That's exactly what you do," he answered. "I know this area better than y'all do. I can get to her faster. And if you draw Linden away, that's one less SSU thug we'll have to deal with."

"Do it," Jesse said quietly from the backseat.

J.D.'s lips pressed flat with displeasure, but he drove on in silence.

As Gideon had hoped, the Buick fell back seventy yards behind them. "As we near the curve, gun it. Then brake when he's out of sight."

The curve loomed closer. J.D. pressed the pedal to the floor and they whipped around the curve at an alarming speed. He braked almost immediately and Gideon flung open the passenger door. He jumped out of the car, slamming the door shut behind him, and rolled into a shallow ditch just off the shoulder of the road.

The Caddy drove on. Gideon stayed flat, out of sight of the road.

Hearing the second vehicle pass, he waited until it was well past before he lifted his head a few inches to make sure it was the Buick that had gone by.

It was. It continued around the curve and out of sight.

Gideon stayed low as he moved, in case there was a trailing vehicle, edging his way deeper into the woods, toward Sycamore Road a mile to the east. According to Rudy's map, the road would take him by an old shack Rudy had labeled "Cody's place." Gideon didn't have a clue who Cody might be, but Rudy had seemed to recognize the place just by Gideon's limited description. And the fact that Craig Linden had been tailing them suggested he was, at the very least, in the right area.

Once he could no longer see the road—and was sure no one on the road could see him either—Gideon stood and started hiking as quietly as he could toward Sycamore Road.

SHANNON'S LEGS WERE cramping from her tightly tucked position. The pain was almost nauseating, but she clenched her jaw and rode it out, keeping a watchful eye on the two men standing just four feet away from her hiding place behind a broken-off pine stump.

"Linden says they're heading well east of here. That old guy must have sent them on a wild-goose chase."

Shannon didn't know what they were talking about, but the grim satisfaction in Leo's tone gave her a squirmy feeling in the pit of her stomach. She could hardly dare to breathe with them standing so close by, and the ache in her muscles and joints was becoming downright excruciating.

Please move on, she pleaded silently. *Go look for me somewhere else.*

"How did she get away from you?" That was Stephens. She recognized the Midwestern accent.

"Ran me into an alligator pit," Leo snapped. "How did she get away from the two of you?"

"She must have found a sharp edge to saw through those cuffs," Raymond said defensively.

"Or maybe you just didn't search her properly," Leo shot back.

She'd be unlikely to hold on to the knife if they caught her again, she realized. They wouldn't let a hiding place in her bra stop them if they got their hands on her a second time.

She had to make sure they didn't find her.

There was a soft burring sound. She gave an involuntary start, afraid she'd forgotten to put the cell phone on vibrate instead of ring. But it was coming from where the men stood.

The sound cut off and Raymond spoke. "Yeah?"

"Give me the phone," Leo demanded.

"You lost yours," Raymond sneered back.

There was a brief scuffling sound. Leo spoke next. "What've you got, Linden?"

Shannon heard the growly sound of Craig Linden's voice over the cell phone speaker. It was almost too faint to make out, but she thought she heard the word *Stone.* She strained to hear more clearly.

"Are you sure?" Leo said aloud.

"The other four people just got out and went into the food mart, but Stone's not with 'em. I looked in the car. It's empty."

"He didn't just disappear."

"I didn't let 'em out of my sight, man. I swear."

"Not even for a few seconds?"

There was a pause on Linden's end of the conversation. "I lost sight for about five seconds around a curve, but I picked them right back up."

The phone in Shannon's bra vibrated, the shock of it knocking about ten years off her life. She folded herself tightly around the humming sound, terrified the others would hear.

"We have to assume Stone got out of the car in those five seconds," Leo said as the phone continued buzzing softly against Shannon's breast. "Where did it happen?"

"Just west of the turnoff to the cabin," Linden answered.

THE PHONE KEPT ringing, but no one answered. Gideon's gut tightened with fear, but he shut off the phone and kept moving forward. He had the cabin in sight. It was almost exactly where Rudy Lawler had drawn it, tucked away in the middle of the rainwashed swamp. A muddy dirt track wound its way through the marsh toward the small clearing where the house sat, ramshackle but still standing after who knew how many hurricanes and tropical storms that had ravaged the Alabama coast over the past few decades.

He eased his way closer, a ghost in the woods, moving with stealth learned through years of Marine Corps Special Operations training. He'd been out of the Corps for two years now, but a marine never forgot.

A quick reconnaissance convinced him the cabin was empty. He stepped into the open and hurried to the cabin, taking it commando-style, in case he was wrong.

But he wasn't. It was empty. There wasn't much left inside anymore—a rickety table, a couple of chairs. On the floor by one of the chairs were the remnants of plastic flex cuffs. They'd been sawed in two.

That's my girl, he thought with a grim smile.

He pulled out his cell phone and tried the number for Leo's phone again. This time, Shannon answered on the first ring. "Gideon, where are you?"

"I found the cabin."

"Get out! They're coming for you!" She sounded out of breath, as if she were on the move.

"What are you doing?" he asked in alarm.

"Coming to help."

"No! Stay put." He lowered his voice, trying to listen for sounds outside the cabin. He heard nothing so far, but if Shannon said they were heading for his position, he believed her. "How do they know where I am?"

"They know you aren't in some car or something—I couldn't make much sense of it." She was whispering now. Did she have the other men in sight? Fear clenched his gut into a tight knot.

"Shannon, find somewhere to hide and stay put. I'll come get you."

"You're outnumbered two to one."

"I'm a marine," he answered flatly. "Being outnumbered is a feature, not a bug. Who's coming?"

"Raymond and Leo."

He edged over to the window and stared through the grimy, rain-streaked glass. He spotted a couple of figures approaching quickly, less than a hundred yards away.

"Have to hang up now. Hide somewhere and stay put!" He shut off the phone and considered his options.

Going out the front door was out of the question—they'd spot him easily. The only choice was the side window, opposite the woods where they were. If he could somehow get them to go inside the cabin, while he was outside, he'd have the upper hand.

The window opened with a loud groan. Wincing at the noise, Gideon vaulted through the window and landed quietly outside.

Even though they'd been moving quickly, they weren't making much noise. But he had to take the risk to close the window. He slid it shut, pleased that it didn't groan nearly as loudly on the way back down. He crept to the corner of the house and crouched low, taking a quick peek through the high grass growing beside the cabin.

There was only one man approaching now. Gideon was pretty sure it was Raymond Stephens. Where had the other man gone?

He edged back toward the wall of the cabin, flattening himself and listening. Stephens was moving with stealth, which would suggest he wasn't trying to draw Gideon's attention away from his accomplice sneaking around the cabin from a different direction. But Gideon couldn't take a chance.

He crept to the back of the cabin and took a quick look. Nobody lying in wait. He slipped around the corner and moved silently along the back wall of the cabin until he had to stop or risk being seen.

Around him, the woods had gone silent. No squirrels chattering, no birds singing. Only a deep, unnerving hush.

Moving with utter silence, trained into him by some of the finest marines to ever wear the uniform, he circled the back of the house and took another quick look around the corner.

Raymond Stephens stood right in front of the cabin, holding a Ruger automatic rifle. He was close enough that Gideon could see the expression on his lean face, the petulant rage that burned in his hazel eyes.

He thinks I'm inside the cabin, Gideon thought, holding his breath to see what happened next.

Stephens answered the question with a rapid spray of bullets straight through the flimsy front wall of the cabin.

THE rat-a-tat of automatic weapon fire split the humid air. Shannon ducked on instinct, crouching in the underbrush as she listened for the sound of bullets whizzing overhead. The sound wasn't immediately nearby, she realized as another round of bullets ripped through the silent swamp. She started to unfold herself from the crouch to get a better bearing on where the gunfire was coming from, but something cold and hard pressed against the back of her neck.

"We meet again." Leo's voice was inches from her ear.

Her heart gave a rolling lurch.

"No greeting in return? Where are those legendary Southern manners I keep hearing about, Ms. Cooper?"

She fought the flood of terror melting her bones. "Your friend's making a lot of noise out there."

"Just getting rid of some vermin."

Gideon, she thought, her heart thudding a rapid cadence of dread. *Please, God, don't let it be Gideon at the other end of those bullets.*

"Let's see, where did we leave off?" Leo asked. "I believe I was going to use you to get the journal. Of course, we'd planned to hold you over your boyfriend's head, which isn't going to work now that it's probably full of lead."

She bit back a moan. Leo was wrong. Gideon wasn't dead. He wouldn't let Raymond Stephens get the drop on him. Not with the warning she'd given him.

He had to be alive.

"Did you know your brother is in town? I have a friend watching him right now."

She started to turn her head to look at him, but he pressed the sharp edge of the gun hard against her skull, making her gasp with pain.

"Maybe we should give your brother a call," Leo added.

So he'd already given up on Gideon? Was he that confident that Stephens had killed him? The unbearable thought nearly paralyzed her.

"Still have my phone?" he asked.

"It's in my bra," she muttered before she could stop herself.

"Give it over or I'll get it myself."

The phone wasn't the only thing in her bra, she realized, hope fluttering through her chest.

"Now," Leo commanded.

She reached under her shirt and pulled the phone free. As she handed it over her shoulder to him, she let the utility knife fall into her palm while he wasn't looking. She took a deep breath and brought her hands together, easing the largest blade open.

"Your brother's phone number?"

"He doesn't know where the journal is. He can't get it for you, no matter how many ways you threaten me." She lowered her hand to her side, the knife blade facing backward. She kept it hidden within her palm, ready for her first chance to make a move without getting herself killed.

"They can find it if they want it enough." Leo pushed the gun barrel against her temple. "Number?"

"Gideon's the only one who knows where it is," she said more urgently. "So you'd better call off your rabid dog out there and pray he hasn't already killed your only chance of finding that journal."

She felt Leo go tense behind her. "You're bluffing," he said.

"You'd like to think so, wouldn't you?" She infused her voice with a cocky confidence she didn't really feel.

But it seemed to work. After a moment of silence, Leo gave her a push in the back. "Walk."

She walked ahead, moving as quickly as she dared without looking as if she were about to make a break for it. If she could just get to Gideon and reassure herself he was still alive, they had a chance of turning this whole mess around on Leo and Stephens.

But long before they reached the cabin, which was barely visible now yards ahead, the gunshots ended. Even as the last blast of the rifle rang in the trees, a dreadful silence swallowed it whole.

Despair rattled through Shannon's body like a chill.

THE RIFLE STUTTERED uselessly, out of ammunition. From his crouched hiding place at the side of the house, Gideon heard Raymond Stephens spit out a string of profane curses.

Time was up. The best-case scenario was that Stephens was out of ammo altogether, but Gideon couldn't count on such a good outcome. He pulled the Walther from its holster and made his move.

Stephens was digging in his pockets, his movements shaky with adrenaline-fueled mania. He found a handful of rounds and tried to shove them into the rifle's chamber. As Gideon came roaring around the edge of the house, he jerked the barrel up and tried to get off a shot, but the rifle jammed.

Gideon hit him with a tackle, grunting with pain as he landed on top of Stephens on the ground. A sharp ache centering around the old bullet hole in his chest made him gasp for breath, but he didn't have time to coddle himself. Stephens was already digging for another weapon.

Gideon stunned him quickly with three hard, fast punches to the face. Stephens's eyes rolled back in his head briefly, long enough for Gideon to flip him onto his stomach and twist his arms behind his back.

Gideon called Stephens a few choice names as he searched the man's pockets. He came away with a Smith & Wesson and a lethal-looking Bowie knife, both of which he shoved into the pockets of his own pants.

Stephens sneered at him. "Big man, what're you going to do? Kill me like your daddy killed your mama?"

Gideon ignored the taunt, digging in the man's pockets for further weapons. He came across a handful of flex cuffs and grinned with grim satisfaction. "This," he said with grim satisfaction as he cuffed Stephens's hands behind him, "is what you call being hoist with your own petard."

"You stupid son of a bitch!" Stephens struggled to turn over, but Gideon slammed his palm against the back of the man's head and shoved his face hard into the ground. Stephens cried out in pain, his voice muffled by a mouthful of mud.

Gideon felt a rush of rage. This man hurt Shannon. He'd shoved her into a car and tried to hold her captive. He'd ripped her watch from her arm, making her bleed. The temptation to shove his face deeper into the mud, to hold it there until Stephens stopped struggling, was damn near overwhelming.

But he resisted it. Instead, he found a measure of satisfaction in fastening the man's ankles together and using a third flex cuff to hogtie his hands and feet together behind his back. Using the cuffs like a handle, he hauled Stephens off the ground and carried him through the cabin door.

"I'll kill you!" Stephens growled, trying to bite Gideon as he threaded a fourth flex cuff through his bindings and attached him to the chain set into the wall.

"You'll have to untruss yourself first," Gideon shot back with a calm he couldn't really feel, not with Shannon out there somewhere, playing hide-and-seek with an armed killer.

He crossed to the window, looking for any sign of the other man who'd been with Stephens. He saw no one out there.

Checking the Walther's magazine, he looked down at Stephens, who writhed with impotent fury on the floor. "Sorry. Gotta go. I'll send someone back to get you." Easing the door open, he took a peek outside.

And stopped breathing.

Shannon stood at the foot of the shallow cabin steps, a gun to her head. Behind her, the man with the gun smiled with loathsome delight.

"Hello, Gideon. I'm Leo. I think it's time we have a talk."

Chapter Eighteen

Shannon locked gazes with Gideon for a brief, electric moment. She dropped her eyes, looking down at the hand with the knife, then looked up at Gideon again.

His eyes narrowed a hair.

"You have something I want, I have something you want," Leo said in a pleasant, almost singsong voice. "I think we can make an equitable trade, don't you?"

"I don't know what you're talking about."

"She already gave you up," Leo said. "She said you're the one who has the journal."

"He won't give it to you," Shannon said, willing Gideon to look down at her hand, where the bright red butt of her knife was peeking out from her fist. But he kept looking at Leo, his expression full of loathing and anger.

"I believe he puts a little more value on you than on a silly book nobody can read."

"He's a marine," she said, dropping her gaze purposefully to her hand again. This time, she saw Gideon's eyes follow her gaze. They slid back up to meet hers, dark with understanding. "Marines don't put anything or anyone before the good of their country. You might as well just shoot me—"

"No!" Gideon jerked his weapon up and aimed it at Leo, his tone frantic. "Don't shoot her!"

She wasn't sure if his cry was heartfelt or an attempt to distract Leo. Whichever it was, it didn't work. Leo just pressed the gun harder into her temple, scratching the skin and making her gasp.

"Why don't we start with you putting down your weapon?" Leo suggested. "Slowly."

Nostrils flaring with fury, Gideon held his gun up and slowly bent, laying it on the steps beside him.

"Where's the journal?" Leo asked.

"It's on the island," Gideon answered. "I can take you to it. Let her go and I'll go with you."

"Oh, no. I know a good hostage when I see one." Leo wrapped his arm more tightly around Shannon's upper body. "Where's my associate?"

"I'm in here!" Raymond Stephens called from inside the cabin.

"He's a little tied up," Gideon said in a flat drawl that almost made Shannon laugh.

Leo did laugh, the sound rumbling against Shannon's back. "I think I like you, Gideon Stone. It's a shame you didn't take a little more after your father, isn't it?"

Gideon's blue eyes glittered dangerously. "I'm nothing like my father," he answered in a tone ripe with conviction. Shannon couldn't hold back a smile, despite her fear.

"Go untie him." Leo pulled his gun away from Shannon's head, waving it toward the cabin.

It was the chance she'd been waiting for.

She slammed her hand backward, planting the blade of the knife deep into Leo's inner thigh. He bucked against her, crying out with pain, and she followed up with a hard elbow jab to his rib. He lost his grip and she scrambled away.

By the time she turned back around, Gideon had rolled to the side, grabbed his gun and brought it to bear on Leo. "Drop it."

Leo stared back at Gideon. "I can't."

"Do it."

Leo swung his weapon toward Gideon. Gideon squeezed off a single shot, hitting Leo center mass. Leo's simultaneous shot fired wide, spraying shards of wood shrapnel where the bullet hit the side of the cabin.

He fell to the ground, the weapon dropping from his hand.

Shannon stared at Gideon, who was still in firing position, his attention focused on Leo's trembling body. Carefully, he crossed to where the man lay, kicking the pistol out of reach.

Leo was still breathing, but bloody bubbles erupted from his mouth as he tried to speak. "I was you…once…" His eyes fluttered shut.

Shannon walked carefully to Gideon's side. He didn't look at her, still staring down at Leo. "Is he still alive?" she asked.

"I think so. Don't know for how long." He reached in his pocket and handed her his cell phone. "Call 9-1-1."

As she started to move away, Gideon's hand snaked out and caught her wrist. He turned his gaze to her, and what she saw there sent a flood of heat coursing through her veins.

"You're the best thing that ever happened to me," he whispered. "When I thought I might lose you—"

She touched his face. "I'm really hard to get rid of. Ask my brothers and sisters."

He smiled at her, flashing those dimples that had first caught her eye. She loved those dimples.

She loved him.

Smiling deep in her soul, she stepped away and called 9-1-1.

SEVERAL HOURS LATER, Gideon sat alone in an interview room at the Terrebonne Sheriff's Department, waiting for someone to tell him what came next. He'd given his statement to Deputy Massey, handed over his Walther as evidence and now sat in silence, deeply aware of being under electronic surveillance.

Shannon had still been on the phone with the 9-1-1 dispatcher when her brothers and cousins arrived, Doyle Massey and a half-dozen deputies in tow. The Cooper men had looked a little let down to see the situation firmly under control without their help.

They'd left the deputies to do the mop-up, encircling Shannon in a cocoon of Cooper family love and protection. Her dark eyes had met Gideon's as the Coopers and a couple of the deputies swept her away from the scene, leaving Gideon to tell a suspicious-looking Doyle Massey everything that had happened.

As they passed, Jesse Cooper's dark eyes, full of meaning, had met Gideon's. He paused a moment, in the chaos, and murmured, "Give me the book."

Gideon hadn't wanted to part with it. But the police would be searching him sooner rather than later. He didn't want the cops to find it.

He reached into his pocket, palmed the journal and handed it over to Jesse in a handshake. Jesse slipped it nonchalantly into the back pocket of his jeans and joined the others as they headed to the nearest Sheriff's Department cruiser.

Gideon wondered if he'd ever see that journal again.

The door to the interview room opened and, to Gideon's surprise, Lydia Ross walked inside, accompanied by Deputy Massey. Gideon smiled at her, relieved to see her safe and sound. He pushed up quickly from his chair and accepted the tight hug she gave him.

"I hear you and Shannon have had yourselves quite the adventure."

He grinned at her understatement. "Yes, we did. Have you seen her?"

He hadn't. Not since she drove away with the deputies in the back of a cruiser. Her brothers had followed in the Caddy, which would definitely need a wash and detailing after today.

"I haven't yet." Lydia took the seat beside him. "I'm so

afraid she's going to disappear without our getting to say goodbye."

"Her brothers want to take her home." Massey stood across the table from them. "But she didn't seem inclined to leave just yet. I just came here to deliver Mrs. Ross safely back to you. You're both free to go."

"No more questions?"

"No, we're piecing everything together pretty well now."

"How's Leo? The guy I shot?"

Massey shook his head. "The paramedics found a broken capsule in the back of his mouth. They're testing what was left of the contents, but it looked like it might be—"

"Cyanide," Gideon murmured.

Lydia made a murmur of distress, and he wrapped his arm around her narrow shoulders.

"They're SSU, aren't they?" Massey asked.

Gideon nodded. "Or what's left of it."

"The Coopers told us about AfterAssets. We'll be turning over Raymond Stephens and Craig Linden to the Feds."

"There's at least a fifth guy, on an Azimut yacht called *Ahab's Folly.*"

"Nobody's been able to find him."

Maybe Damon could give them more information, Gideon thought.

But as it turned out, Damon was gone, too.

"A harbor patrol boat took J.D. and Sam back to the island to check on the chopper," Jesse told Gideon a few minutes later when he and Lydia ran into Shannon's eldest brother outside the interview area. "None of his stuff was left in the lighthouse, either. I guess he swam back out to the boat and they took off."

Gideon swallowed a curse. "I don't think I like that guy."

Jesse smiled wearily. "He's doing a tough job. Being likable isn't at the top of his to-do list."

"Where's Shannon?" Lydia asked.

"Still in there giving her statement." Jesse nodded toward a closed door. "Where are her clothes and things? We thought we'd go ahead and get them so we can head out as soon as they give her the all clear."

Gideon's gut clenched at the thought. "You mean today?"

"Yeah." Jesse gave Lydia an apologetic look. "I suppose we didn't really finish the job we sent her to do. You won't be charged for the time."

"Nonsense," Lydia said firmly. "She worked hard and risked a lot for me. You'll be paid every dime."

"Not until I finish the job."

Gideon's gaze snapped to the now-open interview room door. Shannon stood in the opening, looking bone-tired but beautiful.

"I have more archiving to do," she told Jesse. "I'll stick around a day or two and get that done, then I'll head back home."

"Just because we caught this group of people doesn't mean there won't be others showing up for the same thing," Jesse warned, lowering his voice.

"So let it be known that Cooper Security now has the general's papers," Shannon suggested. "At least if they go after the journal there, you have tons of security and a boatload of trained agents to thwart them." She smiled at Lydia and drew her into a fierce hug. "So glad to see you!"

Lydia laughed softly. "Delighted to see you, too, my dear."

Shannon looked over Lydia's shoulder at Gideon. "You holding up?"

He grinned, ridiculously close to tears at the mere sight of her. "I'm good. You good?"

"I'm great," she said with a grin, making his heart turn a couple of flips.

There was no time for them to speak alone for the next hour, as they returned the Cadillac to the garage and Jesse and Rick joined them on the boat ride back to Nightshade Island.

Worse, Jesse decided to stay on the island as added security, sending his brother—and the general's coded journal—home on the helicopter with their cousins. Lydia offered to open another room for him, but he insisted on taking the sofa.

"It'll be a couple of days before we can leave the island," Gideon warned, slanting a look at Shannon, who shot him a helpless smile. "Tropical Storm Felicia's going to hit late tonight."

"Extra hands to help you bail," Jesse said with a placid smile.

Shannon rolled her eyes and headed up the stairs. "I need a shower."

Gideon did, too. "I guess I'll head over to the caretaker's house and get cleaned up myself," he said to Jesse and Lydia, already on his way out the back door.

He made it halfway through the garden when he heard a soft hiss. Looking up at the second-floor balcony, he saw Shannon standing on the railing, barely visible in the purple twilight, grinning down at him.

"Meet me at the lighthouse in thirty minutes," she said in a loud whisper, her voice carrying to him on the blustery wind. She slipped back inside the house through the nearest French doors.

His heart suddenly pounding an excited cadence, Gideon hurried up the path to the caretaker's house. He bathed quickly and took extra time to shave, brush his teeth and comb his hair. Like a kid on his first date, he thought, grinning at the man in the bathroom mirror.

Night had fallen by the time he started making his way toward the lighthouse, and rain was beginning to blow in from the sea in salty gusts. He wrapped his rain slicker more tightly around him and ran all the way to the lighthouse door.

"Shannon?" he called when he was safely inside.

"Up here." Her voice carried down to him from the top, echoing off the damp stone walls.

He shrugged off the slicker, leaving it to drip dry on the bottom step.

He took the steps two at a time, arriving on the landing with his heart in his throat and anticipation burning in his belly. The door to the service room stood open, a warm golden glow flickering inside, beckoning him to enter.

Shannon stood near the table holding the foghorn control, lighting a second candle. "I thought about just turning on a flashlight and leaving it on, but I like the ambience of candles." She turned around to look at him, a half smile curving her lips. "Alone at last."

She looked beautiful in the most simple, elemental way possible. Her dark hair was still wet, falling over her shoulders in damp strands. Her face was scrubbed clean and glowed like the morning sun. She wore a loose-fitting sundress the color of champagne that nevertheless seemed to hug each curve and plane of her body like a lover.

He'd never wanted anything more in his life than he wanted her.

The burgeoning silence between them was broken by the grumble of her stomach. She laughed aloud, the sound like music. "Guess I should have sneaked us some food from the kitchen."

He laughed with her, closing the distance between them in a couple of steps. He wrapped his arms around her narrow waist and pulled her flush against him. "I'm so glad you didn't leave today."

"Hard to get rid of, remember?" She lifted her face for a kiss, and he obliged, pouring out all his pent-up terror and soul-crushing relief until they were both breathless.

He drew back, cradling her face between his palms. "When I saw Leo standing with that pistol to your head—"

"At least you knew I was alive," she murmured, a haunted look darkening her midnight eyes. "I heard Raymond firing all those rounds, and I thought I'd find you dead."

"I wanted to kill him," Gideon confessed. "It felt like a fire in my belly. I could have dropped him when his ammo gave out. I could have killed him when he tried to pull his second weapon. But I didn't."

She cocked her head, giving him a considering look. "That doesn't surprise me, you know."

He lifted his chin. "I'm not my father."

"No, you're not." She wrapped her arms around him as if she had no intention of ever letting him go.

"You remember when you asked me what I was going to do after Lydia moved away from Nightshade Island?" he asked.

She nodded, her forehead rubbing lightly against his chin. "I do."

He bent and whispered in her ear, "I plan to go wherever you go."

She kissed his throat. "We really are hiring at Cooper Security. I talked to Jesse on the boat trip back here—he's going to let me work on decrypting the journal while we try to track down what happened to the Harlowes. One way or the other, we'll figure out what the general knew."

"I could help. I knew the general. I might see patterns you wouldn't."

"Then it's set." She kissed him again. "I know we barely know each other. I'm not expecting some kind of big declaration or anything—"

"I love you, Shannon." He'd thought the words would be difficult to say aloud, but they weren't. They slipped from his tongue as easily as breathing. "I don't think I can ever stop." He grinned, feeling a little sheepish and a whole lot wonderful. "Hope that's okay."

She laughed. "You big guys don't fall easy, but when you do, it's 'Timber, get out of the way!'"

He kissed her again, desire turning his pulse to thunder in his head, drowning out the keening moan of the rising wind. Only the sound of a voice calling up from below broke through the haze of need. "Shannon, are you up there?"

It was Jesse Cooper.

Gideon pressed his forehead against Shannon's. "I hate your brother."

She laughed. "Give him time. He'll grow on you." She let him go and walked out onto the platform. "Go back to the house, Jesse. I'm fine."

"Are you sure?" Jesse called back.

Shannon turned to look at Gideon, her eyes glowing with happiness. "I'm sure."

He smiled back.

* * * * *

COOPER SECURITY *continues next month*
with SECRET KEEPER,
by award-winning author Paula Graves.
Look for it wherever
Harlequin Intrigue books are sold.

REQUEST YOUR FREE BOOKS!
2 FREE NOVELS PLUS 2 FREE GIFTS!

❖ Harlequin®

INTRIGUE®

BREATHTAKING ROMANTIC SUSPENSE

YES! Please send me 2 FREE Harlequin Intrigue® novels and my 2 FREE gifts (gifts are worth about $10). After receiving them, if I don't wish to receive any more books, I can return the shipping statement marked "cancel." If I don't cancel, I will receive 6 brand-new novels every month and be billed just $4.49 per book in the U.S. or $5.24 per book in Canada. That's a saving of at least 14% off the cover price! It's quite a bargain! Shipping and handling is just 50¢ per book in the U.S. and 75¢ per book in Canada.* I understand that accepting the 2 free books and gifts places me under no obligation to buy anything. I can always return a shipment and cancel at any time. Even if I never buy another book, the two free books and gifts are mine to keep forever.

182/382 HDN FEQ2

Name	(PLEASE PRINT)	
Address		Apt. #
City	State/Prov.	Zip/Postal Code

Signature (if under 18, a parent or guardian must sign)

Mail to the **Reader Service:**
IN U.S.A.: P.O. Box 1867, Buffalo, NY 14240-1867
IN CANADA: P.O. Box 609, Fort Erie, Ontario L2A 5X3

Not valid for current subscribers to Harlequin Intrigue books.

**Are you a subscriber to Harlequin Intrigue books
and want to receive the larger-print edition?
Call 1-800-873-8635 or visit www.ReaderService.com.**

* Terms and prices subject to change without notice. Prices do not include applicable taxes. Sales tax applicable in N.Y. Canadian residents will be charged applicable taxes. Offer not valid in Quebec. This offer is limited to one order per household. All orders subject to credit approval. Credit or debit balances in a customer's account(s) may be offset by any other outstanding balance owed by or to the customer. Please allow 4 to 6 weeks for delivery. Offer available while quantities last.

Your Privacy—The Reader Service is committed to protecting your privacy. Our Privacy Policy is available online at www.ReaderService.com or upon request from the Reader Service.

We make a portion of our mailing list available to reputable third parties that offer products we believe may interest you. If you prefer that we not exchange your name with third parties, or if you wish to clarify or modify your communication preferences, please visit us at www.ReaderService.com/consumerschoice or write to us at Reader Service Preference Service, P.O. Box 9062, Buffalo, NY 14269. Include your complete name and address.

HII1B

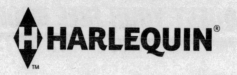

HARLEQUIN®

SYTYCW SO YOU THINK YOU CAN WRITE

Harlequin and Mills & Boon are joining forces in a global search for new authors.

In September 2012 we're launching our biggest contest yet—with the prize of being published by the world's leader in romance fiction!

Look for more information on our website, **www.soyouthinkyoucanwrite.com**

So you think you can write? Show us!

*In the newest continuity series from Harlequin®
Romantic Suspense, the worlds of the Coltons and their
Amish neighbors collide—with dramatic results.*

*Take a sneak peek at the first book, COLTON DESTINY
by Justine Davis, available September 2012.*

"**I**'m here to try and find your sister."

"I know this. But don't assume this will automatically ensure trust from all of us."

He was antagonizing her. Purposely.

Caleb realized it with a little jolt. While it was difficult for anyone in the community to turn to outsiders for help, they had all reluctantly agreed this was beyond their scope and that they would cooperate.

Including—in fact, especially—him.

"Then I will find these girls without your help," she said, sounding fierce.

Caleb appreciated her determination. He *wanted* that kind of determination in the search for Hannah. He attempted a fresh start.

"It is difficult for us—"

"What's difficult for me is to understand why anyone wouldn't pull out all the stops to save a child whose life could be in danger."

Caleb wasn't used to being interrupted. Annie would never have dreamed of it. But this woman was clearly nothing like his sweet, retiring Annie. She was sharp, forceful and very intense.

"I grew up just a couple of miles from here," she said. "And I always had the idea the Amish loved their kids just as we did."

"Of course we do."

"And yet you'll throw roadblocks in the way of the people best equipped to find your missing children?"

Caleb studied her for a long, silent moment. "You are very angry," he said.

"Of course I am."

"Anger is an…unproductive emotion."

She stared at him in turn then. "Oh, it can be very productive. Perhaps you could use a little."

"It is not our way."

"Is it your way to stand here and argue with me when your sister is among the missing?"

Caleb gave himself an internal shake. Despite her abrasiveness—well, when compared to Annie, anyway—he could not argue with her last point. And he wasn't at all sure why he'd found himself sparring with this woman. She was an Englishwoman, and what they said or did mattered nothing to him.

Except it had to matter now. For Hannah's sake.

*Don't miss any of the books in this exciting
new miniseries from Harlequin® Romantic Suspense,
starting in September 2012 and running
through December 2012.*